Bangarang at Carnival

by Osmund James

LMH Publishing Limited

Edited by: Barbara Hall

Cover Design: Susan Lee-Quee

Book Design & Typesetting by: Michelle M.A. Mitchell

Published by: LMH Publishing Limited
7 Norman Road,
LOJ Industrial Complex
Building 10
Kingston C.S.O., Jamaica
Tel: 876-938-0005; 938-0712
Fax: 876-759-8752
Email: lmhbookpublishing@cwjamaica.com
Website: www.lmhpublishingjamaica.com
.

Printed by: Smith's Printing Services Ltd.   ISBN 976-8184-19-1

Contents

Section Three - *Earth's Sexiest and Merriest Show!*

Prologue

He was cleaning his submachine gun. There was a smile lighting his black face, his thick lips parted just enough to show jewelled teeth. He was in one of his west Kingston homes.

He was widely known as Don J, a ruthless gang leader who hated cops as only an ex-cop turned gangster - such as himself - could. On this the first Monday morning of March 1991, he was enjoying the lingering ecstasy of yet another sweet dream of himself and his 'boys' killing cops in great numbers. Lately he had been having such dreams almost nightly.

Don J, sitting in his sun-washed third storey bedroom, cleaning his Uzi and remembering his violently sweet dream, couldn't have known that fate was about to hand him a chance at fulfilling his dream of killing a great number of cops within an hour. A chance to kill scores of cops on the Road March day of the upcoming Carnival Week. And he would be offered a fortune to do the task.

On that same first Monday morning of March 1991, Bishop Brown of the Zealous Pentecostal Church was with his council of elders finalising plans for the protest march he had planned for the day of that year's carnival Road March. Bishop Brown, fondly called 'Pastor' by all and sundry, was telling his council of elders that they were going to need lots of strong sticks in case the 'carnival-sinners' decided to fight. God's chosen people must not flinch from war if it was necessary. Had not the Lord commanded Israel to clear the Promised Land with the sword? Likewise, Pastor concluded, if to stop the sinful Road March from being held on a Sunday meant cracking some skulls, 'backsides' and ribs, then crack them they must! And those carnival-sinners would be the better for it, as the sticks were to be blessed with holy water and prayer.

"And we must keep the real depths of our plans to ourselves; not even our Deacons and wives must know before the appointed mornin' that we will be havin' more than just a harmless protest march ahead of the sinful carnival march ...."

And so, Kingston – the capital city of the Caribbean island Jamaica; a city partly surrounded by rocky hills where the rich prefer to live; a city whose harbour was once one of the loveliest in the world; the city that is the home of Reggae music – was, at the beginning of March 1991, gearing itself for its second big annual Carnival Week, set to begin on Easter Day and to climax with a massive Road March the following Sunday. The 1991 Carnival Week was to be a fun week, as it had been in 1990, even bigger and better. But there was trouble brewing in several quarters.

Yes, Carnival Week 1991 would be lots of sensual fun: but would fate keep the pains and conflicts from causing bloodshed? Would fate prevent Road March day from being soiled by plots of murders and maiming?

Section One:

Introducing ...

Chapter 1

Her heart was pounding. It was nine o'clock on the morning of the first Monday of March 1991. A sunny Kingston morning. She knew Harry was at his work-site by then. But the thought of what he'd do to her if he was to come back unexpectedly and catch her packing to leave him was ... deadly terrifying.

He would kill her. At least dying would be sweet relief from the 'murderation' she knew he'd give her ... in fact she was sure he'd beat her near to death. She could almost feel his huge coarse black hands around her slender black neck, choking out what little life would've remained after the 'murderation'.

Oh sweet Jesus, she prayed silently, please let me get out of Kencot safely. She knew how difficult it could be to escape from this Don J controlled area down-below-Half-Way-Tree, Kingston.

Her loving uptown man was waiting for her at his posh apartment. He loved her. She loved him, but not because he was brown, handsome and an accountant. He was so loving, gentle, proud of his black half, and young ... thirteen years younger than Harry's forty, and just three years older than her twenty-four.

Jenny, the last dress crammed into the larger of her two worn suitcases, closed and locked them. With a sigh, she sat down on the bed. Jesus, please let me get out of Kencot safely. "Mass Joe," she whispered, "come with your taxi."

Ah! Jenny wiped the beads of sweat from her smooth black brow, trying to force aside some of her nervousness.

"Dave darling," she said, "I'll soon be by your side. Come along Mass Joe."

She glanced around the crowdedly furnished bedroom. What a good thing she and Harry didn't have any children. Children would have been a big complication now that she was leaving. She just wouldn't have been able - and never will be able - to abandon any kids of hers. And what a good thing she had always striven to speak proper English, even though many around her were always scoffing at her speech, jeering her as a 'speaky-spokey'. Dave might've accepted her with children, but she was sure he wouldn't have fallen in love with her if she didn't speak proper English.

She could never understand why a ghetto girl shouldn't speak standard English, the official language of the nation. She never scoffed at those who spoke patois. People must be free to speak as they please. And those who called her 'speaky-spokey' were unfair, as she wasn't one of those 'stush' types who used silly accents. Her speech was plain, clear standard English.

"Come along Mass Joe, come with your taxi," was all she could whisper to herself.

Jenny jumped up off the bed in glee. Mass Joe's taxi was honking at the gate. She ran out of the two crowded rooms she had shared with Harry for the past four years. "Coming Mass Joe!" "Ah coming," she called from the verandah and hurried back inside. She heaved the larger suitcase off the bed. It was heavy, but she could manage to sling it two-handed. Coming out of the bedroom into the hall she found Mavis, her nearest neighbour, entering unannounced. She watched as Mavis with a questioning frown on her forehead asked,

"But se' here," Mavis gasped, "is whey yu off to wid suitcase?"

"I am leaving," Jenny said evenly.

Mavis' dark-brown face registered incredulity. "Yu mean leavin' Harry?"

"Yes, and Kencot." She pushed pass Mavis.

"Well, well," Mavis clucked, managing to imply that it would not be long before she would see Jenny crawling back to Harry. She went out behind Jenny.

Mass Joe entered the tenement's small, narrow dirt yard to take the suitcase from Jenny. He was a short, thick-set, middle-aged christian who didn't talk much. Jenny hurried back inside.

"Yu coulda did tell me yu leavin'," Mavis said indignantly from her perch on the verandah rails.

Harry would have heard within twenty-four hours, Jenny thought. She had no intention of quarrelling with Mavis this day. Mavis would just love for them to quarrel before she left. Mavis never lost a quarrel. Jenny fetched the small suitcase, and the travelling bag bearing her three pairs of shoes. Her two worn suitcases and the travelling bag were part of the meagre legacy she had inherited when her mother died six years before.

After locking the door of her former home, Jenny gave the key to Mavis saying "Give Harry. Tell him I say he'd do well to return to his wife in the country." She knew Mavis wasn't a thief, only a gossip and warrior.

"Jus' de other day Harry tell me him goin' seek divorce to marry yu," Mavis announced, falling in step with Jenny.

"Too late."

By this time there were several persons peeping from the tenements next-door and some at the fence of the home across the street. Others moved to take up positions along the fences and street. The poor have a natural knack for sensing strange events: and in the hard times of 1991 it was strange for a young girl to be leaving Kencot for a posh uptown apartment. Holding her head high, Jenny walked ramrod straight towards the taxi.

"Den," Mavis coaxed, "yu not tellin' me whey yu movin' to?"

"Mobay," Jenny lied sweetly. "My man is picking me up on Constant Spring Road."

"A wish yu luck, chile," Mavis said, aching to go spread this latest news along with a speculation that Jenny intended to do 'whoring' in Montego Bay. "Mek' me know how t'ings turn out."

"Of course, my dear." Jenny even hugged Mavis. "Take care." She got into the taxi. Jenny breathed a sigh of relief as Mass Joe drove off. She was leaving a life-time of poverty behind. Her pretty black face relaxed. She was sure of Dave's love, knew he'd love her forever. Neither of them would ever think of leaving the other. She was going to make him happy.

Her thoughts moved back to her mother and their one-room in Jones Town. Her father had disappeared when she was a baby. Her mother had scrubbed floors and clothes to support herself and her one child. Her mother who'd had so much courage, even in the face of the cancer that killed her at forty. And then for the next two years, parentless, she had to put up with her cantankerous grand-aunt because she couldn't find a job. Then she met Harry. He had recently abandoned his wife in St. Mary. Her instinct was against living with a married man, especially one who was more than ten years her senior.

But finding a job was so hard for a girl with her mediocre office skills, especially one as black as herself. So she moved in with Harry. And Harry had been kind enough, which was why she'd remained with him even during the two years she worked as a typist. And she saw to it that he sent money to his wife regularly, good money. He wasn't all bad. She was faithful to him until – Dave. She hadn't known what love was until she met Dave.

Dave was love.

Jenny got out of Mass Joe's taxi on Constant Spring Road. From there she took another taxi to Dave's Hope Road apartment. Mass Joe, she knew, wasn't one for gossiping, but his wife was, and they lived near Harry. It would've been foolish to allow Mass Joe to carry her to Dave's place. She was sure it would be months before Harry would stop wanting to haul her back to his place.

Dave had wanted to fetch Jenny in his car, but she had convinced him it would be best if she came by taxi. Allowing him to come for her would've given Mavis a chance to note his car's licence number. Now, as she drew near Dave's building, Jenny began to wonder if she was dressed right for the occasion at hand. She was sure her form-fitting short-sleeved collarless red dress would stir Dave. He just loved her legs, and the dress was short. But was it wise to begin their home life on such a sexy note?

Why not? Men are so big on sex and Dave is such a skilled lover for his age; at least with my limited experience of young men I always thought only men over thirty knew how to make love. But Dave, ah, he has such a slow easy touch....

Despite herself, Jenny felt heat welling in her core. She touched her low head of curls in a vain effort to stem her arousal.

The taxi turned off Hope Road and slowed instantly, and there he was - her love, her life - standing with the guard at the security box at the compound's barred gate. In her eyes, he looked like a god. Most of his tall, well-built golden-brown body was on show - he was in blue running shorts and matching muscle-vest, against which his sleek muscles seemed straining to escape. She waved, beaming.

She would have smiled even more if she could have heard Dave's enthusiastic remark:

"Here is the lady I am expecting," Dave enthusiastically told the security guard. The guard raised the barrier and the taxi drove inside, Dave, his heart pounding ecstasy, hurried after it.

The compound's small, paved front-yard was bathed with the late morning sunshine. The five storey, apartment building was painted a muted pink, an oblong building just five years old and occupied mostly by young professionals - married, single, unwedded couples, friends sharing a rented apartment. It wasn't a sprawling building - it was a comfortable block which housed twenty two-bedrooms, six three-bed-rooms and ten one-bedroom flats. It was an Hope Road address but the exit/entrance was on an avenue off the main road. It was just a few road miles away from Jenny's former home in Kencot. But by usual standards it could have been a hundred miles, as the surrounding neighbourhood was upper-middle class.

Dave hugged Jenny and planted a firm kiss on her glossy red lips. How beautiful was this diamond-black lady of his. He was so lucky she loved him.

"I am so happy," he said, holding her close. I swear I shall be true to her, he told himself. In this world that's hard for a man to do, but I shall do it.

Gazing into each other's eyes, they were oblivious to the grinning taxi driver. Fighting against the urge to grind her hot pelvis against him, Jenny stood limp in his embrace, loving his tender strength and the hard evidence of his desire. "I am dying to get inside with you," she whispered, "My Dave."

He released her with a sensual grin and heaved the two suitcases from the taxi's trunk. He felt like a giant. This was how Jenny always caused him to feel. How he loved her!

Jenny took the travelling bag from the taxi's back seat and paid the driver as two neighbours from the same apartment block walked by.

"So that's the girl Dave left the Brooke's girl for," said the young lady with the light-brown complexion to her yellow-brown complexioned girl-friend as they got into her shiny new Honda, some forty feet away from Jenny and Dave. Her tone was even, and her accent

9

clearly upper St. Andrew. "Well, actually, Jodi Brookes is so dumb I don't blame Dave, if this one is intelligent. After all complexion and the cut of ones features are meaningless. My pride is in my brain, not my European-like face and brown complexion."

"Only a stupid minority of brown Jamaicans put emphasis on skin colour," said the 'browning' of the yellow-brown complexion. She, too, had an upper class accent. "But sad to say, they give us all a bad name with the black masses."

Meanwhile, Dave had reluctantly given into Jenny's insistence that she be allowed to carry the smaller suitcase and the travelling bag. Dave felt strong enough to carry ten suitcases, and Jenny as well. Lord, he thought to himself, today is the beginning of 'I' man life!

Smiling at each other, he and Jenny hurried inside the building. They floated through the lobby. Kissed and giggled, like teenagers in the elevator.

As soon as they entered the living-dining room of Dave's one bedroom apartment, the lovers dropped their luggage to the carpet and fell into a tight embrace.

I feel like a giant sixteen year-old, Dave thought.

I am the happiest girl in the world, Jenny thought.

He bent his face towards hers. The clash of their lips was both tender and fierce. Bodies crushed into one, they trembled with desire and love and headed for the bedroom.

Dave and Jenny had met on the first Saturday of that year. They had come close to bumping shopping trolleys in the frozen-foods section of the Hi Lo food store on Constant Spring Road just minutes after opening time. (Both hated crowds, so always went to the supermarket very early or very late.) It was Jenny's favourite supermarket; Dave on the other hand was making his first trip there.

"Ooops!" He had exclaimed, dragging back his near empty shopping trolley; he had never out grown his boyish glee for them.

"Sorry, I wasn't paying attention." she gasped, gaping up into his face and wondering why she was blushing and ieeling so much taller than her medium height.

"We were both gazing off at the frozens," he said amiably, conscious of a sublime joy in his soul which was unlike any emotion he had known before. "Of course, I now have eyes for only the most beautiful girl in the world."

Jenny felt her blush deepen, and felt a radiating heat trace over her cheeks and neck, creeping down, down... Being black she knew her eyes were her main give-away, and she didn't want this upper-middle class up-towner to know the effect he had on her. But she just couldn't break the eye contact: it was magnetic, almost cosmic.

They seemed oblivious to the several other early shoppers gazing at them.

"I know I shall never forget this moment," Dave said softly.

She clutched the handle of her shopping trolley tighter, feeling a rush of ecstasy which was beyond mere physical pleasure. With super-human will she forced her eyes away. Away from his brown eyes, and his riveting stare.

Seeing that she was gazing at his T-shirt, and wondering if the magnetism and joy he felt was love at first sight, he said "Like my soca shirt?"

'I SOCA CRAZY' was printed down the front of his white T-shirt. Like her, he was clad in blue jeans. Her jeans were tight, hugging her sexy curves. She wore a loose red blouse which didn't hide the glorious swell of her bosom. His mouth watered.

She nodded, in answer to his question concerning his "soca shirt". She didn't trust her voice. Eyes glued to his sturdy chest, her mouth watered. Her head jerked up at the tremor of his voice when he remarked:

"I love to dance to soca. But at home and night clubs I prefer reggae and the blues." He was embarrassed by the tremor of his tone. What was wrong with him?

She felt exhilerated, knowing, that he too was on edge over this meeting of theirs. But she was sure he wasn't the shy type. It seemed obvious to her that he felt what she did. Could it be love...? He was so handsome. How beautiful were his lips and his flushed brown cheeks added a boyish charm to his face.

"I love soca music," she said sincerely. Her voice was steady, but a bit husky. "Both for listening and dancing. Of course I love reggae music. I even love some classical types."

"You are all the best music rolled into one," he heard himself saying. Where the hell did such a corny line spring from?

But Jenny was beaming to match the sweet warming swell of her heart. She loved his poetic compliment. "I bet you have all the uptown

11

girls eating out of your hands." Why was she saying such silly lines? "I am a ghetto girl, you know."

"You don't sound like the few ghetto girls I know." Like Jenny, he wasn't aware that the supermarket was filling up steadily.

"Born and raised in Jones Town and now living in Kencot." Dear God, why was she telling him these facts?

"Being from the ghetto, uptown or in the hills doesn't make you who you are," Dave said eloquently. "There is good and bad every-where. Many of our worst criminals were born in and still live in the upper and middle classes, many are leaders of the underworld."

She was so pleased with his response she could have kissed his san-daled brown feet. "You a professor or something?" she asked with pro-vocative battings of her eye lids. Of course, she knew he wasn't any form of professor. She was just teasing. He made her feel so sexy and important.

"Just a lowly accountant," he laughed. "And living alone." He found himself quickly replying.

For several seconds they stood beaming at each other across their shopping trolleys, momentarily transported away from the shoppers and sounds swirling about them. They seemed frozen in time, as they were still at the very spot in the frozen foods section where they had almost crashed trolleys minutes ago.

"I am an unemployed typist," she said. Then gulping nervously, she looked away, feeling compelled to add, "I live with an older man."

"But you don't love him." It was almost a statement of finality which he found himself saying.

Several eavesdroppers stiffened, and shook their heads. Jenny's head whipped up to face his. He smiled at her.

"Let's get our shopping done, then finish our conversation," he said, startled to realise how many shoppers had arrived since he and this intriguing, gem of a girl, had started talking. He felt as if he had just fallen from heaven to an earth which was a million times better than he remembered it being. This was when they exchanged names.

As Dave and Jenny shopped together, their intermittent talk was mainly about the on-going price increases, but there was no mistaking the physical and emotional chemistry between them. Each was aware of and warmed to the other's magnetism, content to bask in its joyous warmth.

She was amazed by it all. Usually she was drawn to black men, not golden-brown mulattoes...

Dave had only one medium size bag of grocery when they were through. Jenny had two. Carrying his and the smaller of her two bags, he led her outside to his car after she had refused to let him pay for her groceries.

The sky was slightly overcast. The plaza was filling up rapidly. Cars, taxis, and groups of pedestrians were pouring into the plaza and the other plazas they could see across the traffic-jammed multi-laned Constant Spring Road. Dave placed the two shopping bags he bore onto his Ford Escort's trunk. He took Jenny's handbag and placed it by the other bags.

"Now we can talk freely" Dave said with a boyish grin.

Jenny noticed the slight dimple in his clean shaven chin. Why was she falling for this young golden-brown, part-negro? She looked off to hide her agitation. Why? Jet black men were her usual eye-full.

He noticed her agitation. But more profound to his senses was her glowing beauty out there in the open. An African princess, he thought.

"So what, you taking part in this year's Carnival Road March?"

"No," she replied wistfully. "I wish I could. My man says we can't afford it. Oh, he'll allow us to go to a few of the fetes, but I'd have loved to be in the Road March."

"Time might change all that," he said. The look he gave her made her heart flip. He was envisioning a picture of himself and her in a carnival road march. "I will be in the Road March. Was in it last year."

"It is such a wonderful thing," she said. Feeling more relaxed, she leaned against his car. "God bless the organisers for bringing it here to Jamaica. I used to dream about going to Trinidad's whenever I read about it or saw clips on TV."

"I went there twice and once to Rio's." His voice wasn't boastful; she was aware he wasn't boasting. "Who knows," he continued," you might go many times. They also have some kind of carnival in all the other Caribbean islands and a few North American cities. Perhaps the two of us - as one - might go to many carnivals."

Their eyes locked. Lost, they forgot time and place. Conscious only of their unique ecstasy.

Jenny sucked in her breath at the misty look in his brown eyes. She instinctively knew it was more than mere lust. He was feeling what she felt! Only time would tell whether he could face the reality of loving a not too highly educated girl from the ghetto...

God, Dave was thinking, she was so damn beautiful and majestic... a black jewel... a true diamond-black. Even her name... Jenny, the gem.

She broke the eye-contact: it took a lot of will to break it. Her eyes were warm with love.

They remained silent. Each lost in thought. She was obviously intelligent, he mused, though not highly educated. She spoke well and had a sharp wit... it would be so easy to love her, for ever... something about her was so different from all other girls... but would she feel comfortable in his upper-middle class world?

"I can't stay much longer," she suddenly said. "Have lots of work to do today."

"How are you getting home?" What he really wanted to do was to take her in his arms and beg her to go off with him.

"By taxi." Inside she was shocked to know that what she really wanted was for him to whisk her off to his home. But he was still a stranger, and regardless of the chemistry between them, despite her knowing she was falling in love: Love at first sight?

"Jenny, we know you don't love your man." His voice was gentle, face serious. She frowned up into his face. But her heart was pounding with tingling excitement.

"You and I must meet again soon, for lunch. I don't mean to imply that you are loose or cheap."

"I was never poor. I was born into the upper-middle class, so I can't say I know about being poor. But I do know what it is for a ghetto girl to live with a man because he can support her. After all, many middle and upper class marriages are about money and security; up to a generation ago most wealthy marriages were purely about forming power blocks." He laid a hand on her shoulder. "Can you get away Monday, join me in New Kingston for lunch?"

"Yes," Jenny heard herself saying, eagerly. The sweet electricity of his hand on her shoulder had her floating above her body. "I can usually go out at midday. I have no kids." Was she giving in too easily?

"Fine," he was beaming like a torch in the bushes at midnight. He was going to see her Monday, and she had no kids to complicate things. "We'll meet at twelve o'clock sharp at the Jam Rock Cafe on Knutsford Boulevard, if that's fine by you."

"I know it," she said. "Saw it in passing. Meeting you there at twelve is fine."

"Let's shake on it," he said with glee. He took both her slender hands in his bigger ones, gazing down into her upturned face. Oh how he'd love to kiss that lovely mouth. But she was living with a man and one never knew what eyes were about. "It's a deal."

"You bet." She knew he had come close to kissing her. She was glad he hadn't; yet she wished he had.

"You have lovely hands," he said, squeezing them gently. Jenny's hands were soft and smooth because she went to great pains to keep house-work from ruining them.

Dave hailed a taxi which was cruising over on the other side of the plaza. Jenny came down to earth, suddenly aware of the filled plaza. And the noise!

The taxi arrived. Dave guided Jenny's shapely body inside, then handed her her two bags of grocery. "See you at lunch Monday," he said, shutting the taxi door.

"I'll be there."

Their eyes spoke volumes. The taxi drove off. Jenny looked back and blew her love a kiss. Dave feinted a dramatic catch.

Something told Jenny he had caught her heart. She felt so alive, as if her life was just beginning. It was as if she had recieved a new soul. Yes, she was one of the lucky few who knew love at first sight.

Dave waved, remembering the words of a famous reggae hit of the past: "You've caught me baby, You've caught me girl. And I love no other one but you..."

Chapter 2

Dave and Jenny had thought a lot about each other the rest of that weekend. Each saw, heard and smelt the other via memories of their supermarket meeting. Sharp memories. Sweet vivid memories. Memories which stood out all day and invaded dreams. Ecstatic remembrances of every move, every word, every look, every touch.

At night Jenny pretended that Harry, was Dave. She didn't like doing this, but it was the only way Jenny could bear to have Harry make love to her. To deny Harry sex on weekends was, as bitter experience had taught Jenny, an act of war - Harry rarely wanted sex on weekdays, Mondays to Thursdays; but on weekends, Harry was all for sex unless he was dead drunk; and Harry, who had a tough head was almost never dead drunk.

All day Saturday - after her return from the supermarket, where she had met Dave - and all day Sunday, Jenny was able to day-dream of Dave. Harry was out from morning to dusk both days - out with his friends drinking, playing dominoes, telling rude-jokes and pinching girls.

For his part, Dave was free to dream of Jenny, except for when he visited his parents' Norbrook home Saturday evening and when Jodi Brookes came to his apartment that Sunday afternoon.

Dave and Jodi had been 'steady' for just over two years, and had come close to engagement. He had called it off just three months ago, because of Jodi's vain ways and lack of common sense.

Having known her casually since teenage days, he wasn't surprised

16

at how uninformed she was and that she lacked intelligence, but he had assumed she had some common-sense. How wrong he was. He had known many former beauty queens who were vain, but Jodi was by far the worst. In fact, he came to see her as nothing but vanity. Jodi, the sophisticated former Miss Jamaica, who seemed to think Jamaica would sink if her 'light' beauty wasn't always admired. She had attended a chic Kingston girls' school but had graduated without learning much. She was your original dumb beauty. After her poor show in high school she decided not to bother trying college since she had beauty and a good inheritance. For her life was partying and sex.

Yes! Jodi was a beautiful quadroon with a lovely, thick mass of curly, auburn hair. And she hid from the sun in a vain effort to lose her naturally dark complexion. She was tall, stately, with a pretty oval face and large dazzling eyes framed by long lashes. And good in bed. She easily won the Miss Jamaica beauty title, going on to become one of Jamaica's top models.

She seemed to have been born to thrill men sexually and she loved it.

But Dave preferred intelligent girls. So he had lost interest after basking in Jodi's sexual skills for over two years. He wanted more than great sex from a relationship, and people had begun to expect an engagement announcement.

But Jodi was so dumb and self centered, she just could not accept that Dave had lost interest in her. She was sure no man could resist her beauty and skill in bed. Of course, she had mused, Dave wanted her as his wife and he was the perfect catch for her - young, brown, with an inheritance to match hers, and a rewarding career. On the other hand Dave was down because he wasn't moving super fast in his career, had always expected to outdo everybody, so feeling that Jodi deserved the best, he began to subconsciously feel that he wasn't good enough for her.

So there she was turning up at his door, intruding on his thoughts of Jenny.

Well, Dave was never one to mince words. So although he allowed her inside, he did not allow her to linger. In no uncertain terms he told the glittering Jodi never to return to his door, to go spread her lovely thighs for any of the many men panting after her. "I don't want you!" He concluded. "Keep pestering me and I might smash your face. Scram!"

17

Jodi fled. Terrified. She was sure Dave had gone insane. Dave resumed his pleasurable thoughts of Jenny.

Monday dawned brightly. Especially bright it seemed, to Jenny in Kencot and Dave uptown.

By the time Jenny arrived at the Jam Rock Cafe, few minutes after noon, Dave was already there waiting. The sight of Jenny, in her short peach-coloured, sleeve-less dress, sheer stockings and heels with her face lightly made-up, cap of curls glistening, made Dave glow inside and out. She was the loveliest girl he had ever seen. He almost shouted out this thought. He stood and waved.

Jenny sauntered into the three-quarters full restaurant, oblivious to the lusting men, the rich decor and the low jazz in the background. Dave, looking so sharp - she thought - in a dark-brown suit, pale yellow shirt and light-brown tie, was the only thing which captured her eyes and senses. Even if things didn't work out perfectly, how lucky she was to have met this man.

They beamed at each other as he took her hands, gently squeezed them, and kissed her cheek. How long would it be before he would be able to kiss her lips anywhere, anytime, he wondered.

The contact of their hands and his lips to her cheek sent electric thrills surging from the points of contact to their pounding hearts.

"You look beautiful," Dave said, his misty brown eyes locked with her equally misty dark ones.

"You make me realise men can be beautiful," Jenny said unsteadily.

They blushed simultaneously. Why was he blushing? He wondered, a thing he hadn't done in a decade.

How lovely he was, she thought, realizing that he probably hadn't blushed in years.

There were four, light complexioned young ladies watching Dave and Jenny intently from the restaurant's entrance, wondering who Jenny was. All four were junior management executives at Island Investments and Insurance Ltd. They were in their late twenties, trim, sophisticated and intelligent. Each was single and totally liberated. Bette Fox, so named after the famous actress of the old glory days of Hollywood, was a tall Jamaican white, the oldest of the four, she was also the daughter of Henry Fox, the Chairman-President and major shareholder of Island Investments and Insurance Ltd. Two of Bette's companions, Joan Sams and Dorret Lewis, were mulattoes of the ordi-

18

nary middle-class; the other, Annette Burns, was a quadroon of the upper-middle class.

Since Dave had broken off with Jodi Brookes, Dorret Lewis had been hoping he would fall for her. So it wasn't surprising that she scowled at Jenny's profile and said in cold tones "Who is that black girl with Dave?"

"Definitely not of our set," Annette replied caustically.

"I suggest we give Dave a wide berth," Bette said and floated off towards their reserved table. As always, the other three followed. But Dorret wasn't pleased, even though she told herself that Dave couldn't want more than sex from such a black girl.

By then, Dave had drawn out Jenny's chair and seated her. As he sat, he glimpsed Bette and her three companions/co-workers going towards their table, but pretended not to see them. He had time and eyes only for his lovely Jenny. By that evening, he thought, Bette and her loyal 'Troopers' would make sure their "Yuppie" set knew he was dating a strange black girl.

On one hand Dave liked Bette. She had her false airs but she was intelligent and didn't place too much score on skin colour. She did think being white was a great asset because the world was full of bigotry and because white was synonymous with economic stability. But her closest friends were all part Negro and money was of the least importance on her scale. On the other hand, Dave didn't exactly like Bette's three "Troopers", who had been plodding behind her since high school. The "Troopers" tended to place too much emphasis on skin colour, worshiping Bette's 'total-whiteness' and wishing they had no Negro blood. They looked down on those who were less than fifty percent white and Dave was glad his mulatto parents and most part-white Jamaicans he knew wasn't like Bette's three "Troops".

Dave was as proud of his Negro half, aware that it had taken a lot of spiritual and physical strength for his black ancestors to have survived slavery here in the west, as he was of his white half. He was comfortable with the reality of himself, as he thought all persons should be.

"Should we have a glass of wine?" Dave asked Jenny, as soon as he was seated.

Jenny smiled across the orange table-cloth. "No thanks, I can't bear anything strong during the day."

"Glad of it," he said sincerely. " I am not a great drinker myself, and I have lots of work at the office. I wasn't able to do much this morning because I was dying to see you again."

"So was I," Jenny murmured instinctively, then ducked her head into the menu. It wasn't right to allow a man to see your heart so quickly, she chided herself, even though I am sure he is as much taken with me as I am with him.

Dave picked up his menu. The restaurant's background music and the murmurs of the other diners seeming to blend with his and Jenny's ecstasy.

A military looking waiter appeared at Dave's elbow. He and Jenny ordered.

Dave was pleased with the grace and ease with which Jenny conducted herself. She made the Jam Rock Cafe seem more distinguished than ever, he thought. She was the first black complexioned girl he had ever thought of as more than a friend or lover. Before Jenny, brown complexioned girls had attracted him more, so his 'steady' girlfriends were all brown. Further proof that he was in love at long last, that there was something cosmic about his love for Jenny. Love had nothing to do with skin colour. If Jenny were brown, yellow, white or purple, he'd have loved her just as much.

Chapter 3

After their first date - Dave and Jenny had lunched together at least three times each week, in several New Kingston restaurants. Each date brought them closer and deeper in love. On the Wednesday of the fourth week, Dave secured an extra hour for lunch. He bought take-out chinese and took Jenny to his apartment where they made swift hungry love before eating, then leisurely love after...

Dave was fifteen minutes late returning to his office. But so serene and blissful did he feel, so happily satisfied as never before, that he would have laughed if his bosses had decided to fire him. What 'carnivalian' delight sex with Jenny, his love, was.

That first love-making with Dave was a revelation to Jenny. Of course, Harry had always given her fulfilling sex, usually guiding her to at least one climax. But mutual love, true love, made sex with Dave sweeter and more satisfying than her wildest expectations. Pleasurable agony, ecstatic torture. Colossally wondrous climaxes. Bacchanalian orgasms.

Thereafter, Dave and Jenny's lunch dates took place at his apartment. Usually it consisted of lunch and great sex. Occasionally, great sex and talk, no lunch.

On Jenny's second visit to his apartment, Dave gave her a carnival costume from the same Road March group that he was in. He had recently bought the costume from a would-be reveller for four times its original worth although Jenny didn't know this. He was determined that by Carnival Week she'd be living with him. Jenny was thrilled with the costume but had to leave it at his apartment as she'd have a hard time explaining to Harry where it had come from; she'd have shouted for joy had she known he was aching to ask her to live with him.

Now, on this first Monday of March, eight weeks after their supermarket meeting, Jenny had moved in with Dave, having run-away from Harry at Dave's earnest request and at the pull of her heart. Living together wasn't to be a trial marriage. They were sure of their feelings and knew they belonged together for always, knew they would marry before long.

On this Jenny's first day as Dave's live-in love, they had remained in bed until three o'clock as Dave had the day off. Low soca music flowed from the tape-deck by the bed. The three bottles of champagne which they drank and massaged into their skins sat empty on the bedside table, a testament to their celebration of togetherness. A fourth stood uncovered and ready.

"I guess your first big task will be brightening up my dull flat and making it into our home," Dave said, after their frenzied simultaneous climax of a few minutes before. "I am not good at home making and decorating."

"Most men are not," Jenny said. "But it's not bad, really. Some colour, new curtains, and paintings will do it up fine." She glanced around the bleak, sparsely furnished bedroom. She had always been poor, but she had natural good taste and had learned a lot from magazines and novels.

He took a large swig of champagne. Draping a leg across him, she drank from his lips. Then she laid back on the damp sheets. "What tasty champagne!" She smacked her lips.

"Ah! Tasty with our love."

"We sure are nasty."

"Such sweet nastiness!" They both laughed.

"I didn't tell you before," he said soberly. "Fact is we don't need to pinch pennies. In addition to my salary I have a modest inheritance thanks to my late grand-dad, and I am my father's only heir."

"We must remember you want three kids," she said, touching his nose and caressing his spine.

He kissed her shoulder. "Careful, my diamond-black, or you might not get to unpack before tomorrow."

"Are you superman or what?" Her tone and elevated brows were teasing. "A mean, men can only do so much. Then it's limpness for hours upon hours."

"I'll show you," he growled. She tried to flee the bed. He pulled her

22

back. They tumbled backward and rolled over. Naked and entwined among the crushed pillows and damp, tangled sheets.

When she was calm he felt the first stir of 'new stiffness'. He massaged some champagne into her body and soon they were adding new sweat to the sheets.

While Dave and Jenny were in bed celebrating her move into his apartment, across the city, Mrs. Brown was having an agitated talk with her daughter Carmen. Twenty-three year-old Carmen Brown was the youngest and only girl of three children, and the only one still residing in Jamaica. She shared her mother's alarm.

Mrs. Brown was telling Carmen that her husband, Carmen's father, Bishop Sylvester Brown, the fifty year-old head, founder and prophet of the island's eight-branch Zealous Pentecostal Church, Pastor of the HQ - the biggest of the three Kingston branches, was planning to disrupt this year's carnival Road March.

Mrs. Brown was in awe of her husband and rarely questioned his decisions. But now, as she was telling Carmen, she feared that a protest march just ahead of hundreds of carnival Road Marchers would likely end in a confrontation, as the protest march was to be along the route of the carnival Road March. Knowing the zeal of her brethren, Mrs. Brown feared that they would end up blocking the carnival Road March, causing bloodshed and ruin of her husband.

She didn't tell Carmen, but Mrs. Brown dared not let Pastor even so much as suspect she disapproved of his protest march plan. Whenever she disagreed with Pastor - whether over domestic, religious or other matters - he would put on his black gown, order her to strip and then "whip the devil out of her" with his 'holy-belt'; she always accepted the floggings as righteous, and liked the sex that always followed, but the ensuing day or two of uncomfortable sitting made her prefer to avoid the righteous lashes of the 'holy-belt'.

Mrs. Brown could afford to confide her disapproval to her daughter because Pastor had long ago learned not to become entangled with their "devil-filled daughter". Carmen was a 'carnivalite' and journalist who shared an apartment with a friend.

"He must be getting mad!" Carmen exclaimed, after listening spellbound to her mother's tale of the protest march and its possible consequences. They were seated in the dull main bedroom of her parents' Hughenden home. "I always suspected he was a bit cracked, but this is insanity of..."

"Carmen, please do not forget he is your father and God's servant," Mrs. Brown interrupted, a frown on her brown face. She looked righteous in her roomy dark dress.

Carmen rolled her large eyes, amusement on her dark-brown face. Mrs. Brown chose to ignore her daughter's mockery. Carmen said, "Anyway, we must somehow stop him."

"What can we do? You know his council does anything he says. An' it's all planned already. All eight congregations will be taking part. That means at least eight hundred will turn up. On the surface it looks, harmless, so the police won't tell him to call it off."

Carmen groaned. Knowing her father's influence over his 'sheep' she placed the minimum figure at one thousand five hundred, or three thousand at the maximum "At least carnival is still a few weeks away." She sighed. "I will have to think of some way to stop him."

"Perhaps if your brothers were living in Jamaica they could talk him out of it," Mrs. Brown said, mainly for want of something to say as she wrung her plump hands.

Carmen chose not to voice it, but she knew otherwise. Though older than herself, non-christian and as strapping as their dad, her brothers feared Pastor as much as their short plump mother did. She was the only one who no longer feared the 'Zealous Beast', as she had secretly dubbed him, and he avoided her. He had stopped trying to rule her the day she had moved out on her eighteenth birthday. Before going she had dared to 'blood' his mouth with her heavy handbag. She never knew what had caused her to vent her years of frustration at his zealous paternal rule in such an unseemly manner but something had just snapped inside her and she found herself swinging her handbag at his face.

"Go!" Pastor had roared. "You devil-filled-Jezebel!"

Carmen had fled, pushing aside the urge to apologize because he seemed ready to kill.

"No use," Carmen was now saying to her mother, "no use making a public issue of it. That would only heighten his fervour."

"I don't see how he can be stopped from carrying out his protest march," Mrs. Brown wailed, "I just know it will turn out badly, an' he'll be ruined by it." Privately, she thought the devil had somehow outsmarted her husband this once by putting the protest march idea into his head. "Only the cops can stop him, and most likely they won't out of fear of being accused of being against Pentecostal-type churches."

"Something will work out," Carmen said soothingly. She loved her silly half-crazed mom and hated seeing her so distressed.

"Perhaps you are right," Mrs. Brown said, brightening. "No doubt God will soon tell him it is a mistake." She nodded vigorously. "A mistake to have his protest march along the same route as the carnival Road March and just ahead of it."

"True," Carmen agreed with histrionic enthusiasm. She was sure God had never spoken to her father, and never would. She didn't exactly hate him, though she tended to say she did, but she'd never admit to this fact for more than a fleeting moment. Had she known however, that he flogged her mother she might have considered him public enemy number one.

Carmen was long gone when Pastor arrived home at five o'clock that evening. He was a coal-black giant. Six feet three inches tall, with knots of muscles everywhere. Hands as big as the food trays he loved. Two years older than his wife's forty eight, he looked ten years younger, although he had always worked harder than most two men put together.

Pastor and his wife had been together for thirty years and had both worked hard at building his church group. In the early days as a young preacher, just out of college, he had done construction work and farming to help make ends meet, most of his earnings going into the church. In those days he was living in a rural town and a typical weekday saw him waking before dawn to do two to three hours work on his farm. Then he'd return home for breakfast before heading off to his construction job. By dusk he would be home only to leave again for church or to visit the sick.

Pastor had a voice to suit his size and humour.

"Wife!" He roared as soon as he was out of his car. "The spirit told me our de.il-filled daughter was here today!"

"Yes Pastor," Mrs. Brown said, coming out onto the veranda, not for a moment doubting that the 'spirit' had indeed told him their daughter had visited earlier, "We have to keep prayin' fo' her."

"Yes," he sighed. "She is our biggest cross." He thought again of the slap from Carmen's handbag five years ago. How shocked he had been. She had split his lips. Thank God he had not lost his temper and punched her. "She's our biggest cross," he repeated. "As you say, we mus' keep prayin' fo' her."

"Why worry when we can pray. Seek Jesus an' He will lead the way.

25

Don't be..."

Mrs. Brown joined in the hymn.

Mavis was on the tenement's veranda when Harry arrived home that same Monday evening. Dusk had fallen and it was hot. The unbroken street lights were on. Kencot was alive with evening laughter, curses, music and children at noisy play. The smell of cooking permeated the still air.

"Jenny pack an' gone," Mavis gushed. "Gone."

Harry's big frame came to a jerky halt, his black face frozen with incredulity. Here he was, a forty year-old foreman on a construction site, home after an especially tiring day only to hear that his woman was gone. Gone! God!

Pack? Gone?

"Wha' yu sayin' Mavis!"

"She pack and gone, say she gone to man a Mobay," Mavis said, wary of hinting too broadly, as she had to many women friends, that Jenny had gone to "whorin'". "Gone dis mornin'."

The other residents of the tenement and neighbouring yards, all of whom had already gotten the story from Mavis and had been eagerly awaiting Harry's arrival, were edging closer. Would Harry weep, take blind oaths, smash his home, complain of grave losses?

Harry glared at the onlookers, took his key from Mavis and strode off to his rooms. As soon as he entered he knew it was all true. Too painfully true. Jenny hadn't taken anything she had no right to take. But she had run-away from him.

Run-away from he who loved and had given her so much. He who had saved her from hunger and her aunt's tongue.

Well, I goin' find her sooner or later, Harry fumed as he took out his bottle of rum. I will show her that no woman can make a fool of Harry Jones.

It didn't occur to him that Jenny's running away was not as bad as his desertion of his two hundred and fifty pound wife in St. Mary. And he could not have known that pursuing Jenny would cause him to end up in his own hell...

Chapter 4

By Jenny's third day at Dave's home, his former girlfriend, Jodi, knew he had a live-in lover. A black lover. Jodi herself was being courted by a handsome thirty year-old Jamaican white from the western end of the island and she had no further interest – or thought she didn't in Dave. After all, she was 'near-white' and Dave was 'just' a mulatto. But having weeks ago dismissed the thought that Dave was insane, having reverted to her initial conviction that it was frustration with his dull job that had caused the break-up of their affair, it wounded her to know he had allowed a black girl into his apartment just five months after their split. He had never invited her to be his live-in lover, and that fact rankled.

Never invited me to live with him, Jodi mused indignantly, never invited me during our two years as lovers, but now he has a silly black girl there. Wouldn't be so bad if she was from the upper-middle class or a wealthy black family. But a nobody! I must somehow get at the black bitch.

Jodi resented Jenny with a passion and, on some strange and irrational level, felt she was to blame for the breakup between herself and Dave even though she did not know Jenny and was sure Dave had not met Jenny until after he had broken off with her.

It didn't occur to Jodi that if anyone was to be blamed it was either herself or Dave and not Jenny.

Yes, Jodi mused vindictively, she must somehow get at the black bitch living with stupid Dave. It didn't matter that Dave's desertion of herself had been obviously due to his dull job and slow promotion prospects, which made him think he wasn't good enough for one as white and lovely as her own queenly self. She was going to hurt that black bitch now living with him.

By this time, also, the 'elite' of the Kingston "Yuppies" – they of the upper-middle class, and wealthy families, brown, yellow, red, white and black alike, and their few close friends of ordinary middle class background - knew that Dave had done what some of them saw as the unthinkable: that he was living with an uneducated ghetto girl. Imagine, many thought with astonishment, breaking off with Jodi and then allowing a nobody into your apartment? Jodi was not highly educated and not exactly intelligent, but she was 'somebody', she had status and an inheritance. It was true, Jodi tended to be a bit loose but marriage and kids and a firm hand would take care of that.

If the new girl was one of those pretty educated ordinary middle class girls, or even an educated ghetto girl, it wouldn't be so bad, just as long as she was college educated.

But an uneducated ghetto girl who hadn't even gone to the worst of high schools?

Good heavens, if Dave wanted a black girl why not one from a rich black family? Or any of the well-salaried black career girls from humble origins? Even a nurse or a teacher wouldn't have been half bad. But a dumb ghetto girl?

Of course, there were many elite "Yuppies" – brown, black, yellow, red and white - who were liberal minded enough not to be shocked or affronted by Dave's choice of a black girl. In fact, many of the light-skinned, lady "Yuppies" who were in high paying jobs admired Dave and were glad that he hadn't gone back to Jodi. They knew that Jodi had given him 'bun' left, right and centre and were happy to see him with a decent, albeit uneducated girl.

Bette and her three "Troopers" were amongst the most puzzled. They had been to high school with Dave and had always admired him. Bette was amazed that Dave should seem so serious about such a very black girl - after all, Dave was a 'true' mulatto and could have his pick of the city's most sought after 'brownings' – but far worse to Bette's thinking was that the girl was barely educated. Hadn't even attended high school - what did Dave see in such a person?

28

Bette, Joan and Anette had all had romantic dreams of marrying Dave at one time or another. And all three had allowed him to have sex with them. But now they were only friends.

Bette's fourth trooper, Dorret Lewis, had never had sex with Dave, although she had been in love with him since high school. She had been far too shy and in any case Bette had had a crush on him. Then he and Bette had gone off to a U.S. college and university while she, Joan and Anette attended C.A.S.T. and U.W.I. Bette came back from the U.S. before Dave and by then was no longer interested in him romantically. But when Dave returned to the island he started dating Joan, then afterwards, Anette. When that phase had ended, he fell for a chic older woman, but was soon chasing several young ladies. Next he fell hard for the rich and lovely beauty queen, Jodi Brookes.

Throughout all this, Dorret had successfully hidden the true depth of her frustrated feelings for Dave. She dated other young-men, tried hard to kill her love for Dave, even lost her virginity at twenty-one, but was never able to stop loving and wanting him. Being shy, her hints to him were always vague. Dave either didn't value her charms or never got the message of her unspoken love.

When Dave and Jodi broke up, Dorret's hopes had soared. But once again she had dallied, dreaming and waiting for Dave to proclaim himself smitten with her.

Now he had a black bitch in his apartment, Dorret mused.

"Darling Dorret, why so sad?" Mrs. Lewis asked her daughter on the night of Jenny's third day as Dave's live-in love. Mother, daughter and father were reading in the well lighted sitting area of their middle class, one storey home in Meadowbrook. It was a comfortably furnished home done mainly in muted pastel colours. Mother and daughter were in knee length shorts and sleeveless blouses. "Why so sad, Dorret?" the mother repeated.

"Not sad," Dorret said, forcing a tight smile. "Just thoughtful." She paused to glance at her father seated in the armchair to the left of the sofa on which she and Mom sat. Dad was behind his newspaper. Dorret was not sure she should speak her mind in his presence - he could be such a stuffed-shirt, so unlike Mom to whom she could bare her soul. Although, like her mother, he was a true mulatto he considered himself as black as the blackest Jamaican man and would likely take exception to what she had to say. For a moment, deep-seated malice for

Jenny warred with her fear of what her father would say and won. Throwing caution to the wind she said, "I was just wondering what could have caused Dave to take up with a black girl from nowhere. So stupid."

"Yes, I heard," Mrs. Lewis stated in her crisp, cultivated tones. There was a frown on her roundish face. "Odd. Truly disturbing." She had had hopes for Dave and Dorret, had always encouraged Dorret to pursue him with "lady-like patience". He would be a good catch - brown skinned, an accountant, heir to a tidy fortune, and Dorret liked him greatly.

"Is he on drugs?"

"No," Dorret replied, closing her fashion magazine, "I am willing to swear by it."

"Of course, everyone knows Jodi Brookes is a feather brain. But why drop her and take up a black nobody?"

Mr. Lewis surfaced from behind his newspaper, brown face and receding forehead flushed angrily. He glared at his wife, then at his daughter, got to his feet and stormed off to the library. At times he wished Dorret wasn't his only child, but at times such as this he was glad his bitch of a wife hadn't produced more than one. God forbid two or more of like mind. He should have tried for a child with a mistress, or should've left his wife long ago. Perhaps he should do one or the other before it was too late?

Problem was, Mr. Lewis murmured as he entered the small library, he had been a silly dope to have married an over-ambitious bitch. Stupid of him not to have seen the 'white' ambition under her false humility. She was fifty percent black, had been abandoned by her white daddy but still thought her white half was superior to her black half. She seemed to think whites were gods. Worse, she had passed on her stupid notions to their daughter.

His white father had supported him, even though he had clearly thought his mulatto son wasn't good enough to even look at his white wife and kids.

White, black, yellow, brown or red, Mr. Lewis mused, all were human, some good and bad among all groups. He was fifty-two years; older than his wife, but she made him feel eighty. And much as Dorret frustrated him, he couldn't help loving her. She was the major reason he hadn't left his wife as yet. His wife had shaped Dorret to her suit

30

while he was out labouring at the office. One good thing about the new liberated working woman was that she didn't have the time to meddle with childrens' minds. The husbands of liberated career wives had an equal chance as the wives to mould the kids.

Out in the sitting area of the living-dining room, Mrs. Lewis was saying "Your daddy wasn't always as he now is. I think it's middle-age, and the fact that he hasn't made it as far up as he had wanted."

Dorret had her doubts on both counts. "I can't understand why he failed to admit that blacks are at the bottom of the ladder and therefore should be avoided by our set. Anyway, back to Dave and his new girl."

"A mean, if she was a girl from one of the rich black families it wouldn't be so bad. But a real nobody? Heard that he told friends she hadn't gone to high school, yet they say he claims she is very intelligent. How can anyone who didn't get beyond primary school be termed intelligent?"

Mrs. Lewis couldn't help wincing. She had not gone beyond primary school.

Dorret noticed and said soothingly, "Of course, I don't mean you older folks. Your day was different from ours. High school today is sort of what primary was before the late sixties."

"True," Mrs. Lewis said brightly, "Especially with us girls. In my day it was thought unusual for a girl to be highly educated. Even rich white girls weren't allowed much schooling."

"Thank God for the feminist movement," Dorret said.

"Anyway, I think we should see about setting your cap for another man. No use brooding about Dave. Your thirtieth birthday isn't far off you know." She said reproachfully. She was actually a bit worried about Dorret's poor interest in other eligible men.

"You and your ancient sayings," Dorret said. "'Setting your cap' for a man. Which brings me to say, from his friends' relaying of his avowals, it seems that Dave met the girl just some eight weeks ago, and she ran away from her man."

Mrs. Lewis sighed. "Therefore, as I have said, it is best to put Dave aside."

"No use denying I still like him a lot," Dorret sighed. "And eligible men aren't exactly plentiful. There aren't too many who don't see career girls as threats to their macho image."

"I do understand you young ladies wanting to earn your own

31

money. But all the same it is a bit too much to be saying no babies before thirty. That's partly why young men are running wild until their thirties, preferring to marry girls in the late teens to early twenties. And now this carnival half-naked dancing in the streets..."

"Mom, we will never agree on those points." She grinned. "Same old macho problems."

Mrs. Lewis held up her slender manicured hands in mock surrender. Dorret was the centre of her world and her hope to enter 'high society'; feminist views and carnival Road Marches, were their only differences. They not only sounded alike, but looked like sisters. Both were trim, with light-brown, roundish faces and were of medium height. Dorret's face was more balanced, though, and she looked her age unlike her mother, who, after a life-time of careful pampering and recent plastic surgeries struggled absurdly to pass for thirty-five.

"Our aim is to land you a good husband," Mrs. Lewis said. Then added needlessly, as Dorret desired no other type, "A progressive light-skinned or white man."

"And I do want to marry and have a pair of kids," Dorret said wistfully.

Lying in her bed later that night, Dorret reflected: Perhaps she should have been more forthcoming with Dave after he had stopped dating Jodi. True, Jodi had made no secret that she still saw Dave as hers. But she could've, and should have, invited Dave out on a date, instead of waiting for him to ask her out. All their time together had been spent in the company of Bette and the rest of the gang. Oh, he had danced with her at parties. And at clubs. All types of dancing; he had even kissed her twice.

Why hadn't he gone beyond kissing her at parties? Why hadn't he ever invited her out on a date, just the two of them? She was sure her response to his kisses had been passionate ... well, maybe not as passionate as they could have been but, as Dave well knew, she was a lady.

Damn it, she was sure she had made her feelings very obvious to him many times on the dance-floor. To reggae. To soul and rock. To calypso and to soca.

Perhaps it was because he had been involved with her three close friends?

Whatever the reason, Dorret mused wryly, the fact was she loved him. Thank God, though, her friends had never suspected just how deeply.

Maybe he was the type of man you had to seduce? And she was a liberated girl wasn't she, even though she preferred the traditional practise of the man being both the pursuer and seducer? But before she tried a bout of seduction, she would wait to see if he would soon get rid of that black cur living in his apartment.

Oh how she wanted him...

Her hands crept down to the junction of her thighs.

How many times had she...oh she only knew she had had sex half dozen times in her life.., how she wished she had had Dave even one of those six times... oh how she wished it were his... his hands... his hands now...

Chapter 5

While Dorret and her mother had been discussing Dave and Jenny earlier that night, a Mr. and Mrs. Hurt were seated in the dimly lighted television room of their Norbrook Heights three storey mansion. Their spoilt ten and twelve years old sons were sitting between them watching satellite TV. Both parents were deep in their own private thoughts.

Mr. Hurt was a portly, fifty-five year-old quadroon and sole owner of a chain of department stores. He had inherited a single shop from his daddy but had worked hard to build it up into the seven thriving stores now scattered about the island. He had married for the first time, at the age of forty, to a blonde American woman. They met at a Catholic gathering in her home city of New York.

Mrs. Hurt, now thirty-seven, was still a Catholic, albeit one with a few unconfessed sins under her belt. A beautiful emerald-eyed blonde of ordinary middle-class Catholic background, she had thought Mr. Hurt's wealth and standing in Jamaica would've made up for his lack of passion during their dull courtship. She was a virgin on her wedding night, a virgin with expectations of great pleasure; but it turned out to be disappointing and painful. Then came over fourteen years of sexual frustrations, and two sons whom her husband had spoilt from day one. She had been faithful to her husband until Jamaica's first big Carnival Week last year, 1990.

Looking at the Road March of 1990 with her husband, who claimed to have been keeping an eye out for "wayward" employees in the "Rowdy March" (any he saw, he had said, would be fired for low moral standing), Mrs. Hurt's eyes met one of the handsome dark-brown Road Marchers.

Met and held.

She felt a scalding rush of desire, although he was obviously years younger than herself. It was the first time she ever felt attracted to a younger man.

And what a powerful attraction it was.

The passionate, lusty eye-contact had lasted for no more than five seconds before the reveller was twirled away by two of the scantily clad young ladies of his African-style, costume band, swirling, ranting and raving up Hope Road. (The Hurts were seated in their Benz at the intersection of a residential avenue and Hope Road; their children were home with the live-in maid.) The romantic magnetism of the eye-contact had caused Mrs. Hurt to flush all over - she didn't understand it but was conscious of the various symptoms: thighs squeezed tightly together to hold the heat welling in her core, nipples hard and tingling, face and neck hot with extra blood, heart racing. She had to fight against breathing heavily. And she was alarmed that her husband might have noticed her agitation, her first great fall from grace. To her great relief, a glance across at him showed he was gazing intently out the window on his side - his red ears and neck, bulging pants front, and hard grip on the steering wheel told her his scowl was supposed to be a mask for his delight at the sight of the hundreds of scantily clad female Road Marchers grinding and bumping, to the spine-tingling Calypso music blasting from the sound trucks. He was too wrapped up in his own arousal to notice hers.

Of course, Mrs. Hurt wasn't surprised by her husband's lust for the lady revellers. She had known that his claim to be "on the lookout" for wayward employees was a lie. Just as she had long known that his love for the beaches was comparable to his supposedly secret pornography collection locked in the bottom drawer of his work desk at home.

Donning her sunglasses she relaxed and allowed the lingering sweetness of the lustily magnetic eye-contact to engulf her. She became hotter and moister at the memory.

The reveller of her lust had already moved out of her sight, but she was still seeing his sexy, scantily clad, sweaty brown body. Her junction was turning to liquid fire. It was alarming, sinful, yet unbelievably pleasurable.

"Disgraceful!" Mr. Hurt rasped when the last group of revellers and sound trucks had moved past their car. "This along with the foul reggae DJs means more trouble for the land. At least I didn't see any of my workers." He started the car. His quadroon face was still beet red.

Why bother to pretend with her, Mrs. Hurt wanted to scream at him. Did he honestly think she was so stupid as to fail to see through his facade of moral virtue after so many years as his wife? She had long ago decided that at heart he was an atheist.

As Mrs. Hurt had expected, Mr. Hurt came to her bedroom that night. As usual, it was a fumbling perfunctory action on his part, then he was gone back to his bedroom, leaving her seething with frustration. It wouldn't be so bad, she thought, as she often did following their unfulfilling acts of sex, if he held and stroked her after he had had his satisfaction. (She had once asked him for some fore-play or a good fingering, or perhaps oral sex, before he entered her: his response had been to box her ears and scowl for days.) When was the last time he had kissed her? How many years? Must be more than four years.

Kissing was the one thing he did fairly well - she had taught him on their honeymoon; she had done lots of kissing with her high school boy-friend - but after their honeymoon he began to say kissing was "kids stuff".

Ten minutes after Mr. Hurt's silent departure from her bedroom, Mrs. Hurt allowed her mind to recall the lusty, sinful eye-contact with the handsome young Road Marcher that afternoon. The memory of him was erotic. She saw him, his eyes, his scantily clad sweaty body, that muscular chest.

She felt as if she could almost touch him. Raw pleasure washed her body. Then she was touching the hot triangle between her thighs, fingers tugging at her thick bush... and down, down to her moist petals. For just a moment she remembered her half Jewish mother telling her masturbation was a great sin and could cause her children to be born idiots. She pushed aside the thought. Her second son had ended her child bearing days, and it was then - at age twenty-seven that she had first tried masturbation... But she did it only occasionally, and always told it to her confessor. Sin...oh she didn't think masturbation was a big sin, certainly not half as big as this lust of hers over the handsome reveller she saw today...

36

We all sin, she thought and moved a hand up to her tingling breasts. She lost herself in the pleasure, as in her mind, her hands became his own. She became consumed with surging white heat.

The climax was sweet. And the second was even sweeter. The satisfaction deeper than usual.

Later, before she fell asleep, she tried to understand why her brief eye-contact with the young reveller had so affected her sexually. She could find no answer. It was all unbelievable and inexplicable. Neither could she say why he seemed imprinted in her heart. She was both dismayed and happy over her fall from grace.

The next morning, the live-in maid summoned Mrs. Hurt to the phone just after ten o'clock, waking her from her nap in the den.

"A man on de phone insistin' it urgent he talk to you mam," the maid explained apologetically.

Mrs. Hurt's heart leapt for joy when in response to her "Hello, Mrs. Hurt speaking," a sweet male voice said. "It's your carnival man. What a magnetism it was between us!"

"Who... who are you... how do you know me. I..."

"My name is Cedric Mile. Everyone knows old Hurt and his gorgeous young wife. We, you and I my dearest, must meet today. You put on a hat and sunglasses and come see me, come ease my pain. I live...."

After giving his Jack's Hill address, the mysterious Cedric hung-up abruptly, leaving Mrs. Hurt shaken with fear and intrigue. It was a command she could not, no, did not want to disobey. The memory of their eye-contact was overwhelming. Her need for him was all-consuming and the memory of his voice strongly magnetic. She rushed upstairs, to her room covered her pale blond hair with a wide-brimmed hat, donne ' sunglasses and a baggy sweater. Thank God her sons had returned to school that morning after the Easter holidays. She rushed downstairs.

She drove to her Cedric.

Cedric's home, inherited from his grand-dad, was a neat two storey near the top of a rocky ridge. He was waiting at the open gates. And to Mrs. Hurt's great joy, the carport was at the back of the house. She didn't have to worry about someone she knew passing on the street. Cedric was a twenty-nine year-old bachelor artist/freelance journalist/part-time actor. Son of a mulatto and a black. He gave Mrs. Hurt a most satisfying first lesson. A lesson given to the rhythm of soca.

It was the kind of sex that fulfilled her wildest dreams. The beginning of her year-old sin. A sweet sin. Since then she had visited his house at least once each week. And by the time their lusty passionate affair was four months old she had told him all about her past and her husband's sexual incompetence. In the fifth month, Cedric gave her a black vibrator the same length as his brown, eight inches of hardness. "This will help sweeten your nights," he had grinned at her.

And thus began her second sin with the black vibrator. She had even written 'Cedric' in white down the sides.

Now, on this the night of Jenny's third day in Dave's apartment, Mrs. Hurt - sitting in the semi-dark TV room with her husband and their two sons - was jerked out of her reverie by a shriek from her younger son. She glanced at the television screen. Would she ever be able to spend a night with Cedric? They had never made love at night - nearly a year as lovers and they had never made love later than three in the afternoon, and never before nine in the mornings.

Nearly eleven months of day sex. Always at Cedric's home. And always on week-days. Their love making was never less than titillating and satisfying, but he was the second man she had had sex with - and he was the love of her life - and she would love to know him by night. At times she wished she could go and live with him. He hadn't asked her to, although she just knew he'd welcome her into his home. But she must be realistic. It wouldn't last. He was just thirty and had no children.

I am thirty-seven and unable to bear anymore children, Mrs. Hurt thought bitterly. He will eventually want kids of his own. He will fall for some young lady, marry her and have children. Then I will be able to return to being a good Catholic... keep no other lover and be faithful to my stupid and faithless husband... throw away the vibrator... but for now I am hooked on Cedric's loving.

She sighed mentally. Then brightened at the thought : What fantasy should she act out tonight with her vibrator - her constantly erect Cedric?

How about her and Cedric at a private beach on a moonless night....?

At his end of the U-shaped sofa, Mr. Hurt, too, wasn't watching the movie being beamed from Miami. He was thinking of the magazine his pal had given him today. What a lovely set of heavy-busted, long-legged black girls!

Saints alive! What sex-appeal! Those girls were a delight!

He hoped they had earned plenty cash for posing.

He supposed white girls, had the prettiest faces, Semites the loveliest bosoms, Indians the sexiest hips, Chinese and Japs the cutest bums and feet - but when it came to beauty of complexion and, his favourite, the glory of legs, it was the jet-black Negro girls who took the cup! Black complexion had a glow which was supremely sexy. And nothing, absolutely nothing, was lovelier to behold and touch than a pair of shapely black thighs!

Which reminded him he was to go see that shapely black model tomorrow. But now... the movie was ending, so...

"Boys time for bed," he said, faking a sleepy yawn. "I myself am ready for it." Mrs. Hurt's heart sank. She knew that lustful timbre of her husband's voice. He would visit her room tonight. To breathe in her ear, hurt her breasts and spill himself inside her. All in one swift crude act. His usual "slam-bam-no-thank-you-mam" show.

Oh well, she sighed, at least his visit would be quick. Then she would go bathe, relax and be free to live the fantasy of her and Cedric on a deserted beach on a moonless night.

She got up and followed her sons out of the TV room. Thank heavens for my vibrator, she thought, my perpetually stiff Cedric. And in any case, she never used her vibrator before late at night when she was sure her dolt of a husband was asleep. She was sure he would batter her if he ever saw it.

Perhaps she shouldn't have written Cedric on the vibrator? Oh well, she'd just have to make sure her husband never laid eyes on it. Thank God he wasn't so low as to search her room.

"Come along boys," she called down to her chattering sons. She was at the second floor landing. Mr. Hurt was checking the front door. She added "Let me see you both to your beds." The sooner I do, the sooner your silly dad will come spend himself, and the sooner I will be able to use my vibrator.

Chapter 6

While Mrs. Hurt was putting her rowdy sons to bed, Detective Inspector Hinds was out on the dark balcony of his second floor bedroom smoking a cigarette and looking down on the glowing lights of Kingston's low lying areas. His thirty-six year-old wife was somewhere inside their two storey Jack's Hill mansion. She was a nubile black woman who loved sex, and damn good in bed. To top it off she was also faithful.

But she was a greedy red-eye thing, the Inspector mused, and their two teenage daughters were just like her.

"Poor me, Black Babylon," the Inspector muttered, using the name Rastafarians had given police-men.

He loved sex. And couldn't get enough of his wife's body. She knew how to stir him as no other could. It was because of her that he had taken bribes from smugglers, corrupt politicians and businessmen, and whores and pimps, and stole drugs, to provide her with the luxuries she craved. He was still taking bribes, stealing and selling drugs.

But when a man is drawing near forty, Inspector Hinds thought, mouthing the words soundlessly, his black face frowning in the dark, when a man is drawing near forty you have to take a stock of who you are and where you are heading. How many deaths and how much suffering has my corruption caused?

Of course, Inspector Hinds' well-to-do and rich neighbours knew he was no heir and couldn't have supported his lifestyle without an illegal income. And the more these high society ladies snubbed his wife, the more money she demanded.

He couldn't do without her body, so he kept taking bribes... He loved her; despised her greedy, social-climbing streak, but loved her nonetheless. Now this guilt...

It had surfaced several months before and kept growing. He was from ordinary middle-class origins in St. Mary. Had been an honest hardworking young cop until he met Sonia Green and got hooked on her body and skill in bed. He was then a Detective L/Cpl. and she was a receptionist.

From the very beginning of their relationship, Sonia had not hidden her avid desire for more luxuries than her ordinary middle-class background and job provided: she told him - she wanted to live in a mansion in the hills, her kids must go to the best private schools, she must be able to wear expensive gowns and real jewels, there must be two expensive cars in the carport. His instinct was repelled. But her beauty drew him, and soon the joys of her body and love bound him to her. So he began to take bribes, sell information and steal marijuana. Within two years he was able to buy a three bedroom bungalow in the Kingston eight area and furnish it lavishly, buy Sonia several expensive gowns and a diamond engagement ring. She accepted the ring and moved into his home. The third year saw a Toyota Camry, a Volvo and marriage. Then came a nice bank account. His daughters were soon born. More luxuries. Move up to the hills. More bills.

His corruption kept spreading. And his luck held.

And his love and lust for his wife kept growing.

Sonia's body kept his soul at ease. And he did work hard to solve all sorts of cases. Plus he kept telling himself that all cops the world over were corrupt, he was just one of the smartest and the luckiest.

Another aid to his peace-of-mind was his rapid rise up the ranks of the force. In addition to his hard work on the cases his superiors gave him, the crooks who gave him bribes were also happy to point him into arresting their rivals and troublesome underlings.

Yes, all had been well until the guilt was born several months ago, and had kept growing, threatening to weigh him down.

Now, on this warm, March Wednesday night, Inspector Hinds' reflection was broken by a sudden blaze of light flooding the bedroom behind him and which spilled through windows and door to the balcony where he stood.

"Honey come to bed!" Sonia called from within.

41

Inspector Hinds threw away his cigarette, glanced up at the starry moonless sky, thinking: Tonight was a good time as any to start attacking the root of the problem; he must stop being a slave to Sonia's body. He turned and strode away from the railings. He felt full of purpose. Begin now, he told himself, he wouldn't, must not, make love to her for a week or two. If necessary he must get a full-time mistress.

He froze in the doorway, his heart thudding. His beautiful wife, his darling Sonia, that glorious black body kept trim and shapely by diet and the gym, was on her back on their water bed, her bum elevated on a pillow, knees held to her shoulders, toes pointed at the mirror over the bed, her glistening black thighs spread invitingly to show the heavy lips leading to paradise. She was naked except for the narrow red ribbon laced in her thick blue-black pubic hair. She was all glory. Sexy majesty. It seemed as if she was the source of the light flooding the room. His knees went weak with desire, all his strength centering towards his erection.

No, the Inspector told himself, resist. Resist. Be master of your lust.

"Come to mom boy," Sonia purred, sticking out her long tongue at him and rocking her hips. " Come get your drug, your source of life."

The Inspector felt as if he was steaming in his pants. Balls-on-fire! "Not tonight," he managed to say, wincing at how unsteady and husky his voice was, and so conscious of his red-hot hardness. "I don't feel well." He was still rooted in the doorway and was unable to take his eyes off her. "And it's about time I begin to get more sleep and less sex. I'll soon be forty, you know."

Sonia was grinning. "We both know that even if you are dying you'd get it up when I say so. Right now you are hard as iron. So none of your crap." She spread her thighs wider and reached down to stroke herself. "Come on, run to mom, come for supper."

Resist, resist, go downstairs for a drink....

Instead, he was moving towards her, tearing off his clothes, burning with raw need. His resolve buried under steaming lust.

Later that night as his wife lay sleeping, the Inspector got out of bed to sit in a chair, pondering why he was such a slave to his wife and what he could do to rein in his hunger for her. It is lust for her that helped to make me a corrupt cop. If I could control that, then maybe I'd be able to end my dishonest ways.

Other men desire their wives less over the years. Why is it that I have been desiring mine more.

I am growing old. I believe there is a God. There must be some Great Creator. I'm not sure the Bible is correct, but it is possible that there will be a judgement day, hell and heaven. It's not too late for me to begin to move towards some form of righteousness. I must end my corrupt ways, put more energy into honest work.

Chapter 7

*J*enny woke Dave with a kiss. It was Thursday morning. She
had gotten up long ago thinking happily, "this is my third
morning awakening beside my love". She got quietly out of
bed without disturbing him, showered and began breakfast while he
slept. Now it was seven o'clock. Time for him to begin getting ready
for work.

"Wake up sleepy head," she cooed between kisses to his cheeks.

He opened his eyes with a grin, then flushed with delight at the
sight of her attire. "What, are we to spend the day in bed?" He reached
out for her. She danced away to turn on the tape-deck beside the night-
table. Soca music blasted forth. She began to dance, out of his reach.
He sat up enjoying the show. She was in the skimpy costume the ladies
of their band would be wearing in that year's Carnival Road March, which
was now just over three weeks away. Ah! He and his Jenny would be prancing side by side in the streets. He was glad to see her so happy. She brought
him such joy. And she had done a fine job on the apartment. "My lovely
diamond-black," he cried aloud.

She beamed, loving the term of endearment. "Up Davie-darling,"
she urged.

"It's after seven."

"Yea babe." He got up. "I'd better run go have a shower before a
certain lady cause me to commit rape." He trotted off to the bathroom.

Jenny continued dancing around the colourful, but predominantly blue, bedroom.

Like the rest of the apartment, the bedroom was already a lot more cozy and colourful, thanks to her recent efforts. She had a natural flair for decorating and had spent half the day purchasing tasteful, yet economical curtains, rugs, pictures and other furnishings, at a popular store. Today was a special day for her because that afternoon she'd be starting her exercise program with the famous De.

In the bathroom Dave, too, was thinking of Jenny's first visit to the Fit Centre. Previously he had used the city's most prestigious gym, the Endurance Health Club, but that was where Jodi and Bette and her Troops worked out. He thought it best to keep Jenny away from them as much as possible. So he had signed up himself and Jenny with the fast growing - and perhaps the best equipped gym - Fit Centre. Thank God Jenny was a De fan.

Their goodbye kiss at the front door, forty minutes later, made Jenny and Dave dizzy with pleasure. Each was happy with the other's hypnotic sensual appeal.

Still enjoying the sweet after-effects of his and Jenny's kiss at the front door, still seeing her, smelling her, Dave drove the short journey to his Knutsford Boulevard workplace. His best friend, Joe Hylton, a mulatto, and co-worker drove up just as Dave was getting out of his car.

Joe was one of Dave's few acquaintances who didn't think Dave was stupid to have 'taken-up with' a black ghetto girl: of course, none of Dave's pals who disapproved of Jenny had dared to tell Dave so, as they were all afraid of his Karate skills and temper. Joe was the only friend who Dave had introduced to Jenny. All three had lunched together twice, several weeks ago: after the second lunch, Joe had told Dave "She's witty, lovely and intelligent. The best combination. Best for settling down, that is.

I find it hard to believe she's a ghetto girl who hasn't gone beyond primary school. She's so well-spoken.

My complaint is this - are you sure you are ready for settling down seriously? This city is teeming with sexy career girls without enough university boys to go around. So men like you and I can play the field to our hearts' content. And many of the ladies are prepared to be single moms, so no bar to fatherhood." He paused and sighed. "AIDS is the one problem, but there is condom and no need to eat under the ladies two-foot-tables!"

They had both laughed at that, " I love Jenny more than the Play-boy lifestyle." Dave had explained.

Now the two friends greeted each other, locked their cars and walked into the five storey office block. They were both in light two-piece-suits and tie and bearing briefcases.

Their offices were on the top floor.

"Saturday afternoon you must come visit me and Jenny," Dave said to Joe as they got off the near empty elevator. It was still sometime before the official beginning of their workday. They were extra early because a backlog of work built up recently due to a sick colleague.

"Come give us a boost to face my parents that evening," Dave continued. "They won't say it, but they dislike my love for Jenny because she isn't of our circle. They insist on meeting her Saturday evening."

"Jenny will do fine," Joe said. "Plus parents must not be allowed to intrude on one's love life. Tell Jenny I'll see her at one o'clock Satur-day."

Chapter 8

*J*oe's visit Saturday afternoon did help to soothe Jenny's anxiety over her looming meeting with Dave's parents that evening. She had liked Joe from their first meeting, recognizing that his praise and compliments were sincere. Today they sat around chatting and eating the sandwiches she had prepared along with ginger beer.

It was four forty-five when Jenny and Dave arrived at his parents' home. A richly furnished four bedroom bungalow fronted by a wide thick velvety lawn. Mr. and Mrs. Elliot were both of light-brown complexion. Dave had inherited Mr. Elliot's tall handsome looks but his grandfather's darker brown complexion. Being their only child, the Elliots had been very attentive to Dave but never spoilt him, just as they had never thought it necessary to acquire a multi-storey home in the much favoured hills overlooking the city, a move they could've afforded from the time when Dave was very young. Why a bigger house when they had but one child? they had reasoned, plus the bedrooms were already too much and their flat neighbourhood was a coveted well-to-do area.

Casual, in slacks and shirt, Mr. and Mrs. Elliot were on the roomy veranda when Dave and Jenny arrived. Jenny was dressed in a modest knee-length, jade-coloured dress she had bought yesterday along with its matching low heeled slippers. She wore very little make-up, and gold earrings were her only jewelry. Dave, too, was neat and casually dressed.

Dave made the introductions, silently berating himself for his nervousness.

"Let's sit here on the veranda for a while before dinner," Mr. Elliot said pleasantly.

"Get acquainted with Jenny, so to speak."

They all sat down in the all-white cushioned wicker chairs. From the veranda they had a pleasant view of the mansion-dotted hills at the foot of which the community sat gracefully. "Jenny we brought up Dave to take commitments seriously," Mr. Elliot said in pleasant tones. "So we see your living with him as a serious step. Are we correct?"

Dave was put out, trying to give his father a warning look but unable to catch either his or his Mom's eye. Why the hell was Dad coming on so strong?

Mr. and Mrs. Elliot were gazing intently at Jenny, as if Dave wasn't present.

Without a glance at Dave, Jenny sat up straighter and responded "My mother used to say it's best to take a bull by the horn. I know my ghetto background must be a concern to you, because you love Dave and it is a fact that persons of different backgrounds usually have problems when brought together." She still did not glance at the rigid Dave, her eyes moving instead from one parent to the other. "Dave and I love each other enough to overcome any problem, and have already begun to make the necessary adjustments."

"My one doubt is that Dave is such a wonderful person there is no woman who deserves him totally, least of all myself." She now looked at Dave with all her love, grinned and added "Really, he is so wonderful he deserves to live like those ancient Kings with harems."

Mr. and Mrs. Elliot couldn't help beaming. Dave glowed with proud love, no longer feeling left out.

"Jenny, no offense meant," Mrs. Elliot said. "You speak so well and you don't sound like a girl who didn't go beyond the primary level."

"I didn't get beyond primary and a typing course," Jenny assured her, "but thanks to my mother I developed an early love for reading and speaking proper English. Most of what I know was acquired at the library."

"Jenny," Mrs. Elliot said warmly, "a happy welcome to my home." She took Jenny's hands the handshake turning into a hug.

48

Dave had to blink back tears of joy. Jenny had done the near impossible, won over his suspicious mom in minutes.

"Well this is a good note on which to go in to dinner," Mr. Elliot beamed. "Mrs. Elliot don't hog Jenny to yourself." And so saying he took Jenny's arm and led her inside. Dave and his mother followed.

The middle-aged, live-in-helper was in the panelled dining room, a spacious room with carved mahogany furniture and a gleaming parquet floor. The helper smiled affectionately at Dave before scurrying off to fetch the soup from the kitchen.

The table was set as if for a grand dinner. It was a nine piece dining-set, with a huge bowl of flowers at the end. There were two large seascapes on the gleaming panelled walls. A bank of French windows looked out onto the back garden and pool.

It turned out to be a cheerful dinner. Lots of lively talk and good food. To Mrs. Elliot's and Dave's dismay, Mr. Elliot kept labouring to impress Jenny with his old yarns which they had heard over and over again through the years. Dave was sure that Jenny, like everyone else, found some of the stories corny but you'd have sworn she loved every word. Mrs. Elliot talked about her favourite subject, literature, and was pleased to note that Jenny had read many of the novels she loved. Jenny, in turn, made some humorous quips about the dull state Dave's apartment used to be in, and his pathetic attempts at cooking and ironing. Dave, who was mainly a listener, feigned disapproval while his mother and father mocked him.

"Well just fine," Dave said to Jenny with a playful scowl. "From now on don't you dare say I am behind the times when I sit down watching you work on weekends."

"With you sitting quietly I will be able to do so much more, I have found," Jenny responded.

"Mark your words." Dave chewed a mouthful of chicken before asking "I thought you found my place okay when you moved in? True, it does look better now but I never had any complaints from you before."

"Dave," Mrs. Elliot said, "it was terribly bland, you know, truly bleak, but I never had the heart to say so. So I can understand Jenny's reluctance to harm your ego before now."

Mr. Elliot roared with laughter.

Dave shook his head in genuine wonder at the ways of women.

"Now you are learning what being a man truly is about!" Mr. Elliot chuckled with a pitying look at Dave. "Welcome to the club!"

After the leisurely dinner there were drinks and more talk in the predominantly green living room until half past eight.

Driving home, Dave stopped his car some distance from his parents' house, and turned to a beaming Jenny. "Darling you were wonderful." Then mockingly.

"But did you have to poke fun at me? Such wicked fun it was, too."

They were parked between two powerful street lights on a quiet avenue. Jenny's face was like a jewel in the mellow light spilling into the car. "I'll make it up to you when we get home," she giggled, planting on his cheek a light feathery kiss which had an underlying promise of intense passion.

"In that case you are forgiven," he growled dramatically and drove off.

That night - after watching the video of the 1990 Carnival - their love was a drawn out symphony of tender and passionate loving: quiet bouts interspersed with noisy ones - all agonizingly sweet and done to the low hum of soca music.

When Dave fell asleep, Jenny lay there in his embrace feeling satisfied and happy as never before. The darkness of the bedroom seemed to hold echoes of the sounds of the love-making finished minutes ago. She was the luckiest girl in the world. She had a man who was exceptionally good in every way, and his parents were kind, down-to-earth folks that she loved and who already liked her a lot.

She wished her mother was alive to see her living with Dave. Her father, whether he was alive or not, didn't 'count' because he'd never acted as a father should. Her mother had been the best. She'd have loved Dave. Proud and happy, Jenny imagined her mother's face, smiling at her and Dave, wishing them well, making Dave laugh.

And Dave would've loved Momma, too. No decent humble person could help loving Momma. In fact, Momma would've spoilt Dave rotten, but in a no-nonsense way that would make him even more noble than he already was, she would have loaded him with her good cooking and demand that Jenny treat him like a king. Yes. Dave would've loved Momma.

Momma was never bitter about men, despite being abandoned by the father of her only child. She was always saying that most men at

50

least tried to be good fathers, indeed, many did spend their adult lives being good fathers. Often, Momma talked of the paternal goodness of her own father and grandfathers. "I am just one of the unlucky mothers," Momma had often said, "but I glad I hav' you, Jenny dear, So don't grow-up hatin' man. Pray God to find one of the good ones, an' try no hav' any children before marriage."

Despite their poverty and Momma's tiring jobs, they'd had many happy times. She remembered cooking grand meals they had saved up for, how they amused themselves by telling stories and having riddle contests. She used to sit and read while Momma listened. They would play homemade board games together and occasionally visit their few close relatives. Blessed Momma.

She and Dave would have been that much happier if Momma was alive, Jenny thought fondly, as she slid into sleep, nestling closer to Dave, full of the love she shared with him and willed by the love of a mother which would always echo across time.

Chapter 9

Kingston on Sunday afternoon is a sort of dreamy place. The balmy air, after the scorching heat of morning and midday, is tinged with romance and beauty. The roads are light with traffic and the buses half empty, as it is still too early for that first late afternoon wave of entertainment and spiritual seekers. Those you do see on the roads are all beautiful people, even if they are in tattered clothing. Those heading home are aglow with the anticipation of the traditional Sunday fare of rice and peas cooked with coconut milk, chicken or fish, vegetable salad, and a refreshing fruit juice; while those coming from home are heavy and happy from their meals. Colours are brighter, and people and animals are full of contentment...

Even if the sun is intense, the heat somehow seems welcome to the body and soul.

Yes, Kingston on a Sunday afternoon is a pleasant experience unless...

Bette, dressed in a white jump-suit with an halter neckline to show off her lovely bronze shoulders and new short curly hairdo, picked up her 'Troopers' for their early afternoon Sunday drive. This was an important habit of theirs. All still being single, in their parents' homes and happy-go-lucky by nature, they'd just drive around the city, stopping and visiting where the spirit led them. They sang, laughed, farted, blasted reggae and soca music on the expensive deck in Bette's posh BMW, and flirted with the men they met, not returning home until near dusk.

Today, Anette was chosen to chauffeur Bette's BMW (they almost always used Bette's luxury BMW because it was "the showiest of the four cars"). The BMW's exterior was silver and inside was all fluffy pink and gold. Driving down Constant Spring Road, Anette suddenly disrupted her three companions tone-deaf rendition of a new soca hit : "Hey gang, why don't we give Dave and his girl a surprise visit?"

"Anette baby you are a genius," Bette said, her plain face lighted.

Anette beaming, her quadroon face aglow, tossed her long curly raven-black hair. "So I am captain!" She said with a mock military salute. In her sailor suit and beret she did appear 'navy-ish'; her beret was perched jauntily to the left, her long hair flowing down from under it.

"A surprise visit should knock them for six!" Joan agreed, bouncing on the back seat like a child. She was in slacks and a lace blouse. As always, her face was plastered with make-up. "Let's find out what that black gal is really like."

"Let's hope she doesn't hide from us," Dorret, in a red and white polka-dot dress, said with just a fraction of the hostility she felt towards Jenny. Dorret knew that her companions knew she would have welcomed a courtship by Dave, but she didn't want them to know how hurt and angry she was over his affair with the mysterious nobody Jenny.

Anette increased the speed of the BMW, zooming down the near empty multi-laned Constant Spring Road.

Jenny and Dave awoke a few minutes before noon. It was half past when they sat down to a hearty breakfast of coffee, eggs, toast and orange juice. Then they tidied the apartment before settling down to read - he a Sidney Sheldon; she a Jackie Collins - having decided they'd dine at a chinese restaurant that evening.

"Who could that be?" Dave muttered when the door-bell rang around 2.45. He lay his novel on the nearest of the two lamp-bearing end-tables and got up from the sofa. He ruffled Jenny's curls playfully. "Must be somebody, like Joe, who security knows."

How shocked Dave was when he opened the front door and was nearly knocked aside by the haughty entrance of Bette and her three "Troopers."

53

"Decided to invite ourselves since you don't seem to want her to meet us," Bette flung over her shoulders, sailing down the narrow entrance passage to the living room.

Fuming inwardly, Dave could do nothing but close the door. It wouldn't do to insult those who he had been friends with since school days.

"Why have you switched to the Fit Centre, Davy dear," Anette admonished when he fell in beside her at the rear of the column.

"Time for a change," Dave shrugged. He wished security had called to warn him of the girls' coming, but knowing how sweetly persuasive Bette's tongue could be he couldn't blame the guards.

"Tsk tsk," went Anette. She knew it wouldn't do to goad Dave too much.

Chapter 10

*J*enny was surprised by the haughty arrogant entrance of the tall white girl and her three cohorts. As for that curly headed, yellowish complexioned, near-white one clinging to Dave's shoulder - what gall!

A plastic-smile appeared on the white girl's face as she emerged from the gloomy passage into the sun splashed living room; the drapes and french doors leading to the tiny west-facing balcony were open.

"We are old pals of Dave," Bette said.

Dave hurried up front to make the necessary introductions. Jenny closed her book but remained seated with hands in her lap. She saw that they had made this surprise visit to 'size her up', and believed themselves to be her superior. Well, she'd show them. She'd be as nice or as nasty as they were. She greeted each visitor with a civil nod, saying not a word.

"The apartment looks a lot more homely; I especially love the new drapes, gold is such a sensible colour, and the emerald rug goes well with it," Bette said sincerely, casting her eyes around the sparkling, colourful room. And, she thought, Dave's girl is attractive and does seem confident.

Dorret fumed inwardly as she sat down in an arm-chair. Must Bette pay the bitch compliments? She didn't like the fact that Dave had already allowed the black scum to re-do his home. Next she'd be changing the wall-paper. Was he mad or what? He must be secretly on drugs.

"Jenny's handiwork," Dave was beaming. He was nervously fingering his ripped jeans; Jenny, too, was in ripped jeans and T-shirt.

Bette and Joan flanked Jenny on the sofa. Anette flopped down on a hassock facing them.

Several moments of strained silence followed before Jenny smoothly asked "Can Dave get you ladies anything?"

Bette and her Troopers were clearly startled by the smooth accent and standard of Jenny's English. They had expected... well certainly not someone who sounded almost like the rich black girls they knew, or like themselves.

"Nothing thanks," Bette quickly recovered her wits to say, smiling at Jenny. The Troopers followed their captain's lead, declining Jenny's offer.

Perhaps Dave had been pulling everyone's legs with his claim that this girl was a barely educated soul from the ghetto? Bette and her Troopers wondered simultaneously.

"We heard you are from the ghetto?" Bette ventured bravely.

Dave, standing behind Dorret's arm-chair, winced and was tempted to intervene.

"Yes," Jenny said easily, without delay, fixing Bette with a sincere smile. She had always favoured out-spoken persons. "Born and raised in the infamous Jones Town. Lived in Kencot for the past few years. But being an only child I have no gunmen brothers - of course only a minority of ghetto men are criminals, just as in other classes."

"You don't sound like a ghetto girl," Bette avowed. "Which school did you attend?"

"Your honour," Jenny responded with honest humour," I didn't get beyond primary school and a typing course. But I became hooked on reading from when I was a toddler. Of course, I had to bear a lifetime of being taunted as a "speaky-spokey" which was unfair as I don't use any false foreign accent."

Bette laughed her free-and-easy laugh. Joan and Anette grinned broadly. Dorret forced a smile.

Dave relaxed and went to sit on a hassock next to Joan's end of the sofa. What a fool he was not to have known after her hit with his parents yesterday, that Jenny could handle any attack, friendly or otherwise.

56

"I am beginning to understand why Dave is hooked!" Bette said. "You are witty and interesting."

Jenny smiled, warming further towards Bette.

Dorret was far from pleased with the flow of things. What was the matter with Bette?

"Dave are you all set for Carnival?" She realised it was a silly question once it was out.

"Of course," Dave responded. "Jenny will be a part of our cell. She's training to out-do me. She and I are with the Fit Centre."

"So I have heard," Dorret said, fighting to keep bitterness out of her tone.

"So you are a soca fan?" Anette queried Jenny with raised brows.

"Yes," Jenny responded, beaming. "I especially love to dance to soca!"

"Well," Bette said, "Carnival with its loads of fetes, parties and shows all week is just at hand, a mere two weeks away - wrong, three weeks away."

"I am so excited I can hardly wait!" Jenny exclaimed with what Bette and her group recognised as genuine enthusiasm. (Dorret's spirits sank even lower; luckily she was wearing lots of blusher and red lipstick.) "Last year I couldn't take part. Oh, I am going to dance off my feet!"

This one is a carnivalite and socaphite to her marrow, Bette thought, as bad as Joan and Anette. (Bette and Dorret were average on the scale of soca addiction, they liked the best of all types of music.)

"You have taste!" Anette was unable to stop herself from squealing. "They can dump all other music but leave me sweet, sweet soca!"

Bette rolled her eyes in mock horror.

"I thought all ghetto girls were only crazy over dancehall music," Joan said. "Me, I am soca-soaked-mad!"

Bette and Dave exchanged 'they-sure-are-crazy' smiles.

Seething in her bowels, Dorret had to sink lower in her seat.

"I like dancehall and other reggae," Jenny said. "But only soca makes me hot, hot, hot!"

"Doesn't it!" Anette clapped her hands in glee.

"Soca is the only thing sweeter than sex!" Joan avowed in ecstasy.

Just then the door bell rang. Dave got up and sprinted to the entrance passage. He returned with two casually-dressed, light-skinned young ladies, and immediately noticed that the atmosphere between Jenny and the others was far less warm than when he had left to answer the door. Not that any impolite words had been exchanged. Oh no! It was just a matter of Anette and Joan recollecting that Jenny's love for soca didn't place her in their class or 'set'; Bette was her usual condescending-yet-outspoken-self; Dorret was hiding her hostility behind a bored mask.

Jenny's face lit up at the sight of her two new guests. Both ladies were residents of the building, chic career women, trim and no stranger to Bette and her friends.

"Hello Jenny pie," said Anna-Kay, a petite mix of white and black and Indian. She was a twenty-nine year-old lawyer and from the upper-middle class, "I see you have lots of company." "Hi Jenny dear," said the other, Ruth, a twenty-eight year-old, brown-skinned Negro of ordinary middle class background. She was a loans officer with a major bank. "Bette Fox and gang," she nodded her hello.

Bette and her Troopers smiled at the two new-comers, but were puzzled as to how and when Anna and Ruth had gotten on such friendly terms with Jenny. Jenny had only been here for a week. They were glad that Anna and Ruth weren't close friends of theirs.

"Jenny honey," Anna said, holding up the medium-size paper bag she was carrying, "this morning my husband begged for cheese muffins. I ended up making too many; and Ruth made more carrot ones than her lonely self can manage. So I brought you some of both."

"I don't grudge you and Jenny your men," Ruth said in good cheer. "I can sleep and go out undisturbed."

Jenny and Anna winked at each other.

"So," Dave said, "Jenny has been here just a week and already you ladies are passing me by with your gifts, me, your old neighbour and friend of years."

"My dear sir," Anna said, "we met Jenny in the elevator and one of life's rare super-swift friendships sprang into being."

"And women must look out for each other," Ruth intoned, "with no heed to man, colour of skin, class origin etc., etc." She waved expansively.

Jenny rose and took the bag of goodies. "A thousand liberated thanks to you both."

"There," Anna turned on Dave with an emphatic finger.

Bette never liked being left out. She got to her feet saying, "We have to go now."

"Come and visit whenever you want to," Jenny said politely.

Dave ushered Bette and her thoughtful Troopers to the front door. When he returned to the living room, Jenny, Anna and Ruth were having a lively discussion of their many plans and hopes for carnival week.

Bette left Jenny and Dave's home feeling somewhat warm towards Jenny, though she still tended to think Jenny was after Dave's money. She still thought Dave a fool for falling for Jenny. She could not, though, deny that there was a special magnetism about Jenny.

Anette and Joan felt similar sentiments: But like Bette, neither of them voiced their thoughts.

Dorret had never hated anyone as much as she now hated Jenny, but she thought it best not to allow her friends to know that. So, as soon as they were away from Dave and Jenny's door she steered the others into deep discussion of the latest hit movie.

But the hollowness of Dorret's voice made the others realise that something was amiss and they were sure it had, something to do with Jenny and Dave.

Surely Dorret wasn't in love with Dave? Anette wondered. If that's the case it could prove very sticky.

Could it be that Dorret still had hopes towards Dave? Joan marvelled. It would be bad if Dorret should take it into her head to try to 'save' Dave from Jenny. That would only put Dave in deeper with Jenny and cause Dorret to get hurt.

Good God, Bette thought, it seemed that what they had thought of as Dorret's 'thoughtful interest in Dave' (meaning she'd marry him for social, security considerations) was in fact love she had successfully hidden for years?

Well, well, Bette pondered, it would be interesting to see what Dorret's true feelings for Dave were. She knew Dor was getting eager to start a family, so she would gladly marry a man like Dave even if she wasn't deeply in love with him. Dor's major problem was that she was too demure and old-fashioned about sex. She was sure her friend hadn't had sex even as often as herself and Joan and Anette. Oh, well, Carnival was near, perhaps Dor would get caught up and find a good carnival-lover and forget about Dave.

Chapter 11

While Jenny was discussing carnival week plans with Ruth and Anna, Jenny's former man, Harry, was at his Kencot home thinking dark thoughts of her.

Harry had a strong hunch Jenny was still residing in Kingston city. Regardless of what Mavis had said, he felt that Jenny wasn't far off. He could sense her. And Harry trusted his instinct.

He'd find the bitch. Miss Jenny. Oh yes, he was going to find her.

And when he did find her, he was going to reduce her to Baby Jenny.

Beat the shit out of her. Re-arrange her face and pussy.

Creation of the humble Baby Jenny.

Later that same Sunday evening, Jenny's thoughts as if telepathically, turned to Harry. Ruth and Anna had left in the late afternoon. Then Dave had gone off to see a friend who lived nearby. Dusk was now falling and sitting there alone in the apartment, Jenny began to wonder if Harry had 'swallowed the bait' she had sown via Mavis. Did Harry believe the story that she had run off to Mobay? Or did Harry somehow suspect that she was still living somewhere in Kingston?

Was Harry on the lookout for her, perhaps even searching the city in his spare time? She could almost see him cruising the city in a taxi, wearing a fierce scowl and, looking, peeping, turning to and fro ...

She knew it was going to take him at least a few months to stop wanting to hurt her and begin looking for another girl to live with him. She must be on the lookout for him whenever she went out alone. She'd prefer if he didn't see her for at least six months, but she only feared running into him when she wasn't with Dave. She knew that as big and strong as Harry was he wouldn't stand a chance against Dave's karate skills, plus Harry was very unlikely to bother her if he saw her with a man. Harry was no hero, had more bark than bite where even smaller men than himself were concerned. Harry feared fights.

So she wasn't afraid of Harry seeing her at any of the carnival fetes or in the Road March as she'd be with Dave and there'd be cops around. He wouldn't bother her then.

"Jenny, darling, are you ready to go have a chinese dinner?" Dave called out as he entered the apartment.

Jenny's thoughts of Harry vanished.

"Ready long ago!" She said.

Section Two:

Carnival At Hand

Chapter 12

Dressed in roomy plaid shorts and sports shirt, Pastor Brown tended to resemble what Jamaicans call 'dryland-tourist', meaning one who didn't sail or fly in from across the sea. Pastor was sitting in his study - his sons' former bedroom - and feeling on top of the world. He relaxed in his creaky armchair, his huge bare feet on the gleaming surface of the stained cedar desk. It was a masculine room full of religious books neatly arranged in glass front bookcases. Of course, there were pictures of Jesus and of Pastor in holy attire on the walls. The curtains at the window were a hard brown.

All was set, Pastor mused cheerfully, all was set for rooting out the evil carnival Road Marchers. The Easter beginning of Carnival Week was just four days away. The Road March would be the following Sunday. Pastor was sure that at least two-thousand adults of his eight branch Zealous Pentecostals would turn up for the protest march. They would block the Sandy Gully bridge on Constant Spring Road at his command. Yes, they'd block the bridge even though they would arrive not knowing he'd be ordering them to do so. And he had ordered that parents were not to bring any children under fifteen years-old. They were going to block the bridge for as long as necessary. That would weaken the sinful revelling, as the hedonistic Road Marchers would have to trek a mile or more out of their route to get around the 'bridge-block'. And whichever detour they took, he and his holy flock would move to block that way too. And knowing Jamaicans he was sure the Road March spectators would add to the general confusion with glee, without attacking his flock; any attack would come from the Road Marchers themselves. Though the Road Marchers might be greater in number, they would not be able to force his people off the bridge. They had God on their side as well as the help of the sturdy 'holy-rods' to crack the skulls of the sinful Road Marchers. This sinister aspect of the plan was however, a well-kept secret - only his council of elders, other pastors of the church's branches and head deacons knew the true depth of the plan. The flock and the public thought it was to be a quiet protest march ahead of the carnival Road March. Yes, Pastor Brown mused, he was sure his flock would obey his surprise order. And every man and woman would be issued with a sturdy 'holy-rod' to be used if the sinners tried to force them off the bridge. Plus there'd be an old 'dumpa' truck half full of sand parked across the entrance of the bridge.

Ah, not even my wife knows. He brought his huge fist down powerfully on his desk. The command of the Lord is clear. The carnival organisers must either do away with the disgusting Road March or move it to a weekday or a Saturday. Half naked people dancing in the streets on a Sunday afternoon is sacrilegious!

Detective Inspector Hinds was a worried man.

Although his efforts to lessen his cravings for his wife's body had failed, he had made plans for legitimate investments which would enable him to stop taking bribes in two to three years time and become a 'straight' cop/businessman. So this wasn't what was worrying him now. His present worry was new.

The Inspector's worrying was over having heard, via one of the whores on his bribe list, that a large West Kingston gang was planning a kidnapping and robbery spree which would coincide with that year's carnival Road March. He had heard the distressing news last night.

It was now just three days before the beginning of Easter and Carnival Week. Eleven days to the Road March. To make matters worse, those nosy, mad Zealous Pentecostals were planning a Constant Spring Road protest march a mere half hour before the carnival Road March.

Inspector Hinds sighed and glanced around his drab and cluttered little office at the Half-Way-Tree police station. The grey walls were peeling, badly in need of a paint job since its last one, years and years ago. He was in plain clothes - like most detectives, the Inspector rarely ever wore uniform. It was a cloudy and humid Wednesday morning and

66

there was no air-conditioning in the Inspector's office. Hot, heavy air flowed in and out of the open louvres. His desk fan wasn't much help. He sank lower in the worn swivel chair, closed his eyes, forced aside a picture of his wife's nakedness, and returned to the security problem at hand.

He had told his superior, Superintendent Mills, about the gang's plan for a robbery spree of homes and stores while the Road March was on. The 'Supe' intended to see about detaining as many of the gang members as possible before the Road March. Problem was, it wouldn't be an easy task in so short a time. Half the gang were already wanted for questioning and/or charging. But catching those beasts was no simple matter; they were better armed than the most elite police squads.

Well, the hunting would be in the hands of the special squads, police/military raids and the beat patrols. Their fiery luck.

Inspector Hinds hadn't, though, told the Supe or anyone else about the kidnapping part of the news. For more than one reason. One, kidnapping was nearly unknown in Jamaica, so his informant might be unwittingly spreading a hoax. Don J, leader of the gang the informing whore had mentioned, was a smart ex-cop. Probably the whole thing was a ruse to hide some bigger plan - a bank robbery, an attack on a police station or a mass movement of guns and coke.

Secondly, the Inspector reasoned silently, the informing whore hadn't heard who was to be the kidnapped victim - only that the victim, would be snatched out of the Road March. So the case was wide open. If he could get the name of the intended kidnap victim, or prove it was partly a hoax, it should be enough to earn him command of the case and promotion.

No, the Inspector told himself, he had no intention of putting the intended kidnap victim at risk because of selfishness. He intended to take a crack at finding out the name of the supposed victim Don J had in mind. If by next Wednesday he had neither learned the name nor proved it was a hoax, he would inform the Supe about the kidnapping angle.

Chapter 13

Driving to the Endurance Health Club in the Kingston five area on Wednesday afternoon, Jodi looked very sweet in skimpy black tights which brightened the paleness of her quadroon complexion. Her thick auburn curls blew about her pretty face and creamy smooth shoulders like a halo.

Yes, Jodi looked as sweet as the sunny Kingston afternoon. One would have thought she was surely the source or cause of the cooling wind.

But her thoughts were far from sweet.

She was gloating about the plan she had set to 'fix' Jenny. Last night she had taken eighteen year-old Carl Azee, a Jamaican Lebanese neighbour of hers, to a motel and had given him two hours of her sensual skills. As she had expected he ardently promised to be her instrument of vengeance in exchange for more sex, after he maimed Jenny. Carl had glowed even brighter when she hinted that if he did well she might leave her fiáncee for him.

As if she would want an eighteen year-old boy!

Poor thing had been worshiping her for years and would kill the P.M. if she told him to. No doubt he would be masturbating daily with her on his mind, unable to touch his school girl lovers, until their next coupling after carnival.

She chuckled at the memory of Carl's tears of joy at the sight of her beautiful nakedness, his clumsy trembling hands and four quick rides. He had used his tongue rather well, though.

Come Road March, Jodi hummed, come quick. Carl was going to fake an accident with his spear. He was going to blind one of the black bitch's eyes. Then, ah, we'd see if Dave would want the one eyed Jenny.

How lucky that she, Carl, Dave and Jenny were all in the same spear wheeling African styled costume cell, Jodi murmured as she braked behind a mini-bus.

Harry was still fuming over Jenny's desertion. Vowing to find and discipline her. Every day he was surer and surer that she was still in Kingston.

And there was Mavis goading on his wrath, encouraging him to find the two-timing tramp.

Harry was sure he or some friend would spot Jenny somewhere in the city. Knowing how much she loved soca and carnival he was sure he would be able to trap her during Carnival Week.

At the same time that Jodi and Harry were vowing their respective vengeances against Jenny, Harry's strong agile two hundred and fifty pound dark-brown wife was over in St. Mary under an overcast afternoon sky practising her now competent lassoing skills on her fifteen year-old son and two year-old daughter. She was getting better every day. She was sure she wouldn't miss Harry if she just got one clear lasso-shot at him in the crowd watching the Road March.

A friend of hers had seen Harry and a young girl watching last year's March. Well, this year she was going to fix his business.

The bastard had run out on her and their children five years ago. Not even bothering to return for a visit. He never wrote either.

True, at irregular intervals he sent money via the bank. Impressive sums of money. But money wasn't everything. Oh no!

She hadn't been able to learn where in Kingston he was living. But she was going to catch the bastard at this year's Road March.

For better or for worse the Parson had said, till death do them part. He belonged to her. And she didn't like to commit adultery.

She had no intention of troubling his girl, so long as the girl kept out of it. Her intent was to lasso Harry if she couldn't get near enough to hold him. Pitch him down, sit down on him, truss/him up and, bring him back home.

And she'd have the new 'supple-jack' now soaking in coconut and 'oil-a-stay-ya' oils.

Into her mind came a vivid picture of Harry tied spread eagled to her bed, naked, with herself 'riding' his manhood, boxing his ears whenever he stopped thrusting upward.

She saw a series of vivid pictures of herself and Harry having sex in various positions, as they used to before he ran away. Then she saw him giving her her first experience of oral sex, her thighs engulfing his face.

This last picture of Harry 'eating under her two-foot table' made her giddy. For over ten years she'd been wondering what oral sex felt like, but she'd never dared to ask Harry to do it. But as soon as she brought him home she was going to demand that they try it. It seemed that all the younger lovers were doing it, so there must be some fun in it.

When she brought home Harry, he'd be under her control completely, bound to do her will and to stay with her forever. Beating him with her 'supple-jack' soaked in 'oil- a-stay-ya' would see to that.

Chapter 14

By that same Wednesday night, Carnival Week - especially the Road March climax - and the expected protest march, were the talk of Jamaica. Discussed in every community, on every corner, in every home. The Zealous Pentecostals protest march was seen as harmless amusement by the public. The Road Marchers and carnival organisers weren't alarmed since the protest march was scheduled for half an hour before the scheduled 12.30 start of the carnival Road March, and because the carnival organisers had a secret plan to delay the start of the Road March by up to two hours.

Like all other carnivalites taking part in the Road March, Jenny and Dave were glowing with joyous expectation, anticipating, a ranting, raving Carnival Week. And they were on a strenuous last lap of exercises for fit bodies to endure the nightly fetes and hectic Road March.

".... 21, 22, 23, 24..." Dave was keeping time as he and Jenny did leg lifts on the carpeted bedroom floor. It was after eight and the windows and curtains were open allowing in a slight breeze. They were both in colourful gym wear exercising in time to the soca music piping from their CD player.

".. 30.. 31.. 32.. 33.. 34.. 35." They paused, took deep breaths. Dave said "Now up for cooling down phase."

They stood and put their sweaty bodies through a mild series of mark-timing and graceful stretches.

"Well, my love, that's it for tonight," Dave said, grinning down at Jenny. They slapped palms and touched fists. Since Jenny moved in they had rapidly become best friends. He picked up a towel and tenderly dried her sweaty black brow and neck before doing his.

"I never would have dreamed of such exhilaration," Jenny beamed..

"My exact thought," Dave nodded. "I feel like a giant, and I know having you makes me the luckiest devil alive. I love you my sweet Jenny, my lovely diamond-black."

For a moment they stood there poised, just inches apart, not touching. He gazing down into her bright upturned eyes. Then, slowly they glided into a tight sweaty embrace.

"I love you my handsome devil," she sighed. "There never was or will be any girl as lucky or happy as I."

As one, their sweaty bodies fell to the carpet. They laid there stroking and squeezing each other, loving their sweaty smells, basking in the low tones of soca music. Their love was endless. The night, their love, the soca music and their dreams of a happy future, blending into a blissful oneness.

Dave was thinking that there was no need to delay asking her to marry him. Already, he saw her as his wife. Now he envisaged her as his bride dressed in white with sparkling jewels, as beautiful and arresting as soca music. But he suspected that, though she'd say yes to his proposal, she would secretly wish he had waited a while longer until his parents could have no further doubts about their love. Plus carnival was only days away and would encroach on the intimacy of their engagement.

So, Dave thought, I shall wait another three or so weeks before popping the question if I can wait that long.

Jenny was hoping Carnival Week would push aside Dave's desire to propose marriage. More than once over the past few days she had sensed he was aching to propose. Of course, she wanted to be his wife, and knew he'd be an attentive, dedicated husband. She pictured their wedding in some beautiful garden - a soca wedding; he, so handsome in an elegant carnival costume to match hers, their guests in carnival costumes as well. Yes, she wanted - longed - to be his fiancé, his wife.

But, she would prefer if he didn't propose just yet. She had tactfully hinted as much. She wanted his parents to first realise that his love for her was real: she knew she had won over his parents and that they no longer had any doubts about her love for Dave. Yet they still had doubts about the depth of Dave's love for her. She wanted them to be her parents at heart - so she wanted everything about their engagement and marriage to be acceptable to them.

As for their living together, Jenny knew Dave's parents were not so old fashioned that they didn't accept 'shacking-up' as a respectable way of courting amongst the younger generations.

Dave ended their reverie with a light teasing kiss. Then he said "Honey you got me by the balls and the heart."

Jenny giggled. "I am just as badly tied, if not worse. You've got me by the heart, my nipples and my clit!"

Dave chuckled and drew her down tighter to his chest. "Let's go have a carnival bath," he said.

"Wonder what that means?"

"Rant, rave and misbehave in the bath!" He sang, to the beat of the soca on the CD player.

"Grab a certain hot pulsing thing and wave!" she rejoined, mischievously.

Chapter 15

Wednesday night saw Bette's 'Troopers' sleeping over at her house, a regular week-day happening. Bette was the youngest of the Foxes five children - three boys and two girls - and she was the only one still in her parents' three storey seven bedroom mansion in one of the wealthy havens of rocky Stony Hill overlooking Kingston city from the north. On week-days Bette and her girls had the run of the second floor with its three bedrooms and Bette's mini-gym. Mr. and Mrs. Fox – he a native white; she a chestnut haired British - lived on the third floor. On most weekends, though, the whole house came alive with the shrieks and laughter, of their fifteen grand children. These much anticipated visits never failed to bring a gleam to old Mr. Fox's unsmiling face and 'taut' smiles to Mrs. Fox's 'many-times-lifted' face.

Tonight, after dinner, Bette and her Troops spent an hour in her abstractly-muralled mini-gym. Then they lay their sweaty gym-wear clad bodies on the carpet to sip tonic water.

"Really, I am beginning to wonder if Obeah exists," Dorret said pensively, wiping her weary brow. "A mean, one just cannot understand Dave mooning over an uneducated nobody."

"She is self-educated, Dorret," Bette said with cocked brows and thoughtful eyes. She splashed some tonic water over her bronzed face. "And I am beginning to suspect that somewhere along the line you have fallen head-over-heels for Dave."

"Not exactly," Dorret responded evasively, wishing she had not brought up Jenny and Dave. Still, she added timidly "After he and Jodi

74

broke up it did occur to me that he and I might be suited for each other."

"And now?" From the grinning Joan, her face glowing yellow under the bright lights.

"I am just amazed by his folly," Dorret responded, forcing a sigh and feigning nonchalance. It was a good thing she was a born actress - she should have tried Hollywood instead of Finance.

"It really is very odd," Anette agreed after a few moments silence, frowning thoughtfully. "And I did expect you and him to hit it off real serious."

Bette, never one to mince words or be vague, said "Well, we have all had our Dave 'periods'. First me, then you two , and now Dor." She grinned wickedly at Dorret and added "But Dor is the only one who never 'juiced' him."

Dorret blushed. Her companions rolled about with laughter. Dorret gritted her teeth while they laughed. Anette playfully nudged her with a foot.

"Dor are you sure you'd want to marry a man who has been 'juiced' by your three closest friends?" Bette asked seriously.

"I trust you girls," Dorret said softly with downcast eyes. Then with a big gulp of air she looked up into Bette's eyes and continued, "so if he and I were to marry it wouldn't bother me. After all, you guys are just friends now. What's past shouldn't be allowed to rule the future and present. Influence, as a sort of scale, yes, but not dictate."

"Well said!" Bette exclaimed and they slapped palms all around. "Men," she added, "might allow such things to affect their friendships because of mistrust. We liberated sisters must be more trusting and trust-worthy."

They high-fived again.

Dorret thought it necessary to add the lie "It's not that I was nursing any longtime love for Dave, neither was I all starry eyed after he left Jodi, but I just thought we'd be suited for growing together towards love." She was already madly in love with him, she thought. "I am nearing thirty and it seems I am the type who doesn't fall easily, so a man I like and have known for long, such as Dave, would do me just fine. And he could always leave after we have a kid or two."

The others had their doubts over the truth of this statement. They thought she was deeply in love with Dave, but tactfully decided to keep quiet.

"Somebody give us some soca music," Bette said to break the ice. "Carnival is in the air. Some soca before my bath and eight hours of sleep. And, Dorret dear, it isn't too late for you and Dave."

"I'll get along fine without him," Dorret said with a shrug and brave smile, feeling a swell of gratitude. Surely she had the best of friends, she thought. And since it seemed Dave wasn't about to tire of Jenny in a hurry, she'd try seduction; 'juicing,' as Bette would have said. She must take drastic action before the black bitch tried a fast one on Dave by getting pregnant or something. Next week Saturday, day before the Road March, her parents would be off to the country for the day. She'd invite Dave over, alone., and give him a proper 'juicing.'

Soca blared forth from Bette's large twin-speaker deck sitting squatly by the open windows. Anette had finally selected a tape from last year's carnival.

Chapter 16

Holy Thursday dawned bright, and clear. The bun-and-cheese-taste of Good Friday/Easter holidays was in the air and mingled with the spine-tingling expectant thrills of Carnival Week. At 9 o'clock, Mrs. Hurt was driving to see her lover. She knew it was a 'wicked thing' for a Catholic lady to be doing, especially on a Holy day. In fact she had planned not to see him until after Easter.

But, dear Lord, she had to see him.

Yesterday he actually told her he wanted her to leave her husband get a divorce and marry him. What bliss it would be to do so! But she wasn't sure she could, as it might mean having to give up her Catholic faith. So, she'd asked him for a week to think about it, and he had agreed.

Oh, what pure golden bliss it would be! Nights of exquisite ecstasy!

But could she switch to a protestant faith if she were to be kicked out of her Catholic one? And would he really, as he had avowed, be contented with adopting children?

Mrs. Hurt was now stopped by traffic lights.

She could hear his voice when he had said "Your not being able to bear any more children doesn't affect my love. We can take one of your boys, or both, and adopt others. I love you, my golden heart."

Mrs. Hurt quivered with delicious pleasure at the memory of this avowal.

Mr. Hurt had an early lunch that Holy Thursday and then headed for the Fit Centre.

Recently he had joined the city's top four gyms (visiting one or two most days), having come to realise that next to beaches, Kingston gyms were the place to meet and see the sexiest sights of this world. Those lovely bodies in those fantastic gym-wear! Very, very sexy – a real turn-on.

And, he had been to beaches all over the world, from the south of France to California, from the Caribbean and South America to the Pacific islands, but nowhere did he get as much delight as from the beaches of Jamaica, especially near Kingston. Now the city's gyms were running a hot second place....

Jenny, too, lunched early Holy Thursday and headed for the Fit Centre. For the past three days Dave had been putting in over-time at work so he would be able to go in late for the four working days of Carnival Week. In the taxi, Jenny's thoughts turned to Bette and her 'Troopers,' and that beastly Jodi. Why were some people so stupidly class and colour prejudiced?

Dave, Jenny mused, was right to have secretly dubbed Bette and her three friends as 'Bette and her Troopers'. Bette wasn't so bad for a white girl, especially seeing how wealthy her parents were. She and her Troops were never openly unfriendly the way Jodi was whenever they all met at their Road March group gatherings to practice 'walking-and-whining' to calypso. There were twelve costumed groups of roughly three hundred persons. Each group was sub-divided into three cells and prizes were to be awarded to those groups, cells and leaders who were deemed to be best, by a panel of judges.

Jodi used to be Dave's girl, Jenny mused, so her attitude was a bit understandable because it was Dave who had dropped her. Still, why did she have to be so openly hateful, especially now that she had a new man? And why must Bette and her Troops seek her out to treat her to doses of tactful snobbery? Why wouldn't they all, just leave her alone?

She wished they weren't all in the same cell. She wished she was in the same band as her two new friends, Anna and Ruth. The thought of them brought a smile to Jenny's lips: Anna and Ruth were college-educated and highly respected in their "big" jobs, but treated her as an equal because they liked Dave and were broad-minded.

With a sigh, Jenny returned to the problem of Bette, her 'Troopers' and Jodi.

She had no intention of asking Dave to take action. She must solve her problems on her own. She wouldn't complain to Dave about how annoying she found them. She wasn't about to runaway from their challenges, either. She'd continue giving "tit for tat" confident they'd wear out long before she was near the end of her patience.

"I am glad, though, that Dave left the Endurance Health Club and signed us up with the Fit Centre," Jenny mumbled as the taxi neared her destination.

Like the Endurance Club, the Fit Centre was in the New Kingston area. Jenny got out of the taxi just as Mr. Hurt steered his Benz into the gym's small car-park. He gave Jenny's trim shapely black legs a lip-smacking glance, his eyes popping behind his sun-glasses.

Jenny was in a skimpy gym-wear top, mini-skirt, thick socks and gym shoes. The bottom of her gym suit was in her sports bag.

"Isn't she the girl I have seen with Dave Elliot several times these past weeks?" Mr. Hurt asked himself as he parked his car in the half full concrete-paved car-park. Heat waves shimmered above the pavement. The midday sun was blasting out of a near cloudless sky - and not even a hint of a breeze stirred the leaves of the mango trees under which most of the cars were parked.

Her gym bag slung over her shoulder, and usual sweet smile on her pretty black face, Jenny entered the Fit Centre's front-yard with a jaunty step. Another hour of aerobic dance and floor exercises with the witty De and the other members of her afternoon class. She was an hour early but looked forward to biding her time by watching or talking to any of the friendly, ladies who frequented the Fit Centre.

"Hello there young lady!"

Jenny, startled out of her thoughts, turned to see Mr. Hurt waving and beaming at her while locking up his Benz. Jenny was sure she did not know this portly greying man - white, she wondered, or near-white? - who had hailed her and was now beaming at her like a school boy. Obviously a lecher, she thought but stood her ground and replied "Goodday sir." One can never be sure about middle-aged men.

"Please hold up a second." Then he was coming towards her. He bore down on her grinning foolishly, while obviously fighting to hold in his immoderate paunch. "Name is Mr. Hurt, owner of Hurt and Sons stores," he said sticking out a hairy paw. Jenny took the offered hand; he imprisoned hers gently. "I've seen you with that boy Dave Elliot several times. He is one lucky young man."

"Thank you sir," Jenny said. She wished he wasn't wearing sunglasses. A man's eyes usually tell a lot about his soul, and morals. And she didn't like the hot clammy feel of his fleshy hands. He wore his clothes well though, she saw: he was in striped pants and a plain short sleeve shirt. "I am Jenny, and I have found many bargains in your stores," she added sincerely.

"Glad to hear it!" he exclaimed, releasing her hand after a final squeeze. "I am new on the gym scene. Come twice a week during either the lunch hour or late evening, mostly evenings. You an old timer here?"

"No sir," Jenny said as they headed toward the gym's colourful open front doors.

"So you and I are fresh feet," he said, stepping in time with her. "We must help out each other, right?" He was swinging the plastic shopping bag bearing his gym gear.

"My class is at 1.15 sir."

"No problem." He waved expansively. "You'll find that old Hurt can make anything work in this island. Would be easy, for instance, for me to see your boyfriend in a better job or anything else."

Was this a threat, Jenny wondered, the beginning of this lecher's attempt to blackmail her into his bed? She made no comment and again wished his sun-glasses were off.

They entered the long, airy well-equipped main room of the Fit Centre. There was a bank of eight foot mirrors at one end, in front of which two large aerobics classes were sweating to soca music. Most were housewives getting fit for carnival. In addition were other women and a few young men working out on the various machines. The walls were, brightly painted - a cheerful accompaniment to the huge paintings of athletes here and there. A broad section of folding doors led to a spacious backyard with a pool and outdoor equipment.

"I use mainly weights," Mr. Hurt told Jenny as they paused just inside the entrance.

"I am into aerobics," Jenny said.

"Well, I am going to change right away," he said and headed for the changing rooms. He was feeling mightily pleased with himself, knowing he had her puzzled. Next step will be the loving father figure, then seduction by charm, money or force.

Jenny was headed towards a friendly mulatto housewife working out on one of the treadmills. Could Mr Hurt cause Dave to lose his job or something similar?

"I see you are in high company today," Mrs. Lindo puffed when Jenny was alongside her. She was a tall shapely thick-thighed thirty-seven year-old mother of three. She and Jenny had had several long chats since Jenny had began training there. "But you don't seem too pleased?"

"He obviously isn't an angel," Jenny said. "Called me up outside. Said he has seen me several times with my boyfriend."

"He is known as a 'closet' lecher alright," Mrs. Lindo chuckled and reached out to switch off the treadmill.

"I don't like such men," Jenny said with a forced smile, "but I guess I can bear him here at the gym as long as he doesn't get lewd."

Grabbing her towel from a chair, Mrs. Lindo mopped her sweaty face and neck. "Oh, his type - the respectable church-goer - keep their hands quiet in public.

What he'll do is begin by cultivating a friendship, then start making promises as well as lunch and dinner dates. For the grand finale he will declare his lust. And heaven help you if he sees an angle from which he can blackmail you into bed."

Jenny had to grit her teeth to suppress her dismay. Could Mr. Hurt harm Dave's career?

Mrs. Lindo, picking up on Jenny's distress, asked, "Is anything wrong Jenny?"

Jenny deciding to trust the likeable Mrs. Lindo, replied, "I think he sort of hinted he could help or hurt Dave."

"The nerve of him," Mrs. Lindo bristled in low tones. "Don't be fooled my dear. Dave's father might not be as wealthy as dirty old Hurt but he is no walk-over. And Hurt has, no sway over Dave's career. Dave's workplace is publicly held. Plus Dave can get jobs anywhere. Don't let Hurt fool you with his big talk.

"In fact you can scare the life out of him." She lowered her voice and leaned closer to Jenny's ear. "Seeing that you're from the ghetto, he'll quake in his shoes and pants if you tell him you have several gun-tooting brothers."

Jenny instantly fell for the idea. She grinned at Mrs. Lindo.

"Here he comes," Mrs. Lindo whispered," and I think he's heading straight for you, my dear." She winked at Jenny.

Jenny returned Mrs. Lindo's wink, with smile.

Mrs. Lindo liked Jenny a lot, and she was sure that it would be in Jenny's best interest to get rid of Mr. Hurt as soon as possible. But Mrs. Lindo also would love to see Mr. Hurt squirm, as a small revenge for the way he had abused her friend's two daughters: he had blackmailed the sisters into going to bed with him together, an act that had had a negative effect on the girls, reducing them to nervy recluses.

Watching Mr. Hurt strutting towards her, ideas began to fill Jenny's head.

Chapter 17

Mr. Hurt had emerged from the changing-room strutting in his silk boxers and a loose T-shirt, Bobby socks and red gym shoes completed the ensemble. He had a towel thrown rakishly around his neck and was wearing his 'father-christmas' smile that usually melted young ladies of all colours and classes. His eyes saw nothing but Jenny. He thought her the most beautiful and sexiest 'thing' he had seen in years.

"Ah, Mrs. Lindo, isn't it?" Mr. Hurt said and giving her a swift once over. "Wife of the eminent Dr. Lindo." Half his attention was focused on Jenny.

Mrs. Lindo nodded.

Mr. Hurt was now without his sunglasses and Jenny observed the narrow gleaming eyes which seemed to suggest a soul given mainly to lust.

Mr Hurt turned fully to Jenny. "My new friend hasn't changed as yet, I see."

"I don't begin until quarter-past-one," Jenny said. Another look into his eyes confirmed her opinion of him. He was a man filled with pure raw lust, but appeared relatively harmless otherwise. She pitied his wife.

"How about keeping the old-man's company while he fights with this torturous equipment?" He said to Jenny. It was an unctuous plea.

"I'm off to talk to Mrs. Chin," Mrs. Lindo said, referring to a half-Chinese lady across the room on an exer-cycle. Jenny nodded and smiled goodbye to Mrs. Lindo.

Mr. Hurt sat down on a nearby bench, smiling at Jenny, and said "Now come tell me about yourself. You seem the type of girl this old-man wishes were his daughter. I have two sons, no daughters. I'd give all my money for one though" He sighed.

Jenny drew closer, pretending concern. "I'm sorry to know it's like that," she said.

"My wife can't bear anymore kids, so I must be contented with fussing over young ladies I like."

"Why not adopt a little girl?"

"Funny thing is," Mr Hurt lied with dramatically grave nods, "whenever I think of a daughter I see her as nineteen to twenty-eight or so, although my sons are much younger. And my wife doesn't like the idea of adoption.

I am fifty, so I could've had a thirty year-old daughter." (Long ago he had decided that fifty was an age that stirred young ladies, so he'd stopped counting birthdays as of five years ago and was sure he'd pass for fifty many more years ahead.) "Anyway, enough of my sentimentality. Tell me where you're from and so on."

With a dead-pan face, Jenny said "I'm from Jones Town."

Mr. Hurt reddened. "You must've left there when you were very young?" Hopeful tones.

Jenny hadn't missed either his alarm or the hope in his voice. "I lived there until I met Dave," she answered evenly.

Despite his efforts to hide it, Mr. Hurt was obviously dismayed. He was deadly afraid of running afoul of gunmen from the ghettoes. All those guns. He was a man of peace. He deplored violence. But this girl was so sexy, had such majestic thighs. "You don't sound or look like a ghetto person," he ventured timidly.

Jenny was enjoying herself but kept a bland face. "The result of my nine brothers insisting I be a lady a man like Dave would want," she said with relish. " One slip of the tongue, one bad report from a teacher," she lowered her already low voice so there was no danger being overheard, "and I'd have to sit on several guns until my butt was sore. M16 rifles," Mr. Hurt couldn't stop himself from gulping, his Adam's Apple quivered, "submachines, shot-guns, pistols. And they'd be ready to shoot any man who was unlucky enough to look at me twice. Even after I entered my twenties."

"They don't know Dave but they approve of him because he is a profes-

sional and from a respectable family. You can say they even loved him."
She rolled her eyes dramatically.

"Heaven help the man who tries to come between Dave and I, or tries to harm Dave."

Mr. Hurt jumped to his feet. He was beet red. He didn't doubt Jenny's story. As sexy as she was, he told himself, he could only hope she'd one day fall for him on her own account. "I should begin on the treadmill," he muttered. "Don't think your background affects my immense liking for you. We're friends. If you ever need help, please call on me first."

"I will, sir," Jenny grinned, fighting back laughter. "The things I just told you are secret, You're the only person I've told."

"Of course," he said, hastily." Wouldn't think of telling anyone." He mounted the treadmill none too steadily, cursing his luck. What a loss. And to think most people thought that a rich man had no hardships. Here was the sexiest "woman" he'd seen in years but he dared not apply any pressure to get her to bed. Cops and gunmen he preferred to avoid. Still, hopefully some day Jenny would want him as a lover. Those thighs and that rear of hers ... His eyes went across to where Jenny, Mrs. Lindo and Mrs. Chin stood talking. God, those legs of glory...

While Jenny and Mr. Hurt were talking at the Fit Centre gym, Pastor Brown's daughter, Carmen, was brooding over a light lunch in a crowded cafeteria downtown. It was near to the newspaper *The Gleaner* where she worked. She was thinking about her father's much publicized "protest march". On the surface it seemed harmless enough.

But she had a gut feeling that her father and his council of elders had a secret card to play. Something sinister. She was sure of this but hadn't even told her flatmate of her fear and her suspicion.

"I must somehow get my Zealous-Beast-Of-a-father to call off his protest march," Carmen mumbled. Her thoughtful frown made her dark-brown face suddenly look older than her twenty-three years. "That's the only way to make sure our Road March isn't disrupted, and prevent all hell from breaking loose."

Carmen and her flatmate Natasha Bailey occupied a cramped two bed-room flat on the ground floor of a small three storey apartment building on Red Hills Road. The building had no elevator or security service, but was air-conditioned. The girls had been best friends since high school. Both had college diplomas in Mass Communications. Natasha entered the advertising field and seemed set for a fast climb to the top, just as Carmen was seen as a young journalist with great promise. Their apartment was neat and done in light shades, complemented by the many colourful cushions they had made themselves. They liked reggae and US pop music a lot, but loved soca even more, and were both avid carnival fans.

Carmen was the first home that Thursday evening, and while preparing dinner her thoughts once again turned to her father and his planned protest march, thoughts along the same lines that she had brooded over at lunch. She had to find a way to force her father to call off his protest march. She had to find someway to "blackmail" him - that was the only thing he would take seriously. She was sure he had a secret plan which could ruin the Carnival Road March.

The problem was, Carmen mused, unlike most preachers and most men her father was without vice. "Straight." He was a faithful husband. His followers had to literally beg him to use church funds for the meanest of comforts - the simple house in Hughenden, one of the later housing areas, was church property on "life-time-lease" to Pastor and Mom; his car was church property. Since she and her brothers left home he had cut his salary to near nothing. Despite his huge size and strength and booming voice, he was gentle. He was truly honest, a kind man. His only flaw was in thinking he was "God's Black-Prophet" sent to save the world.

The door-bell rang, ending Carmen's musings.

"What's going down, girl?" The tall vivacious Natasha asked the moment Carmen let her into the apartment. Night was about to fall and Natasha held a bag of groceries, mainly bun and cheese for the holidays at hand. "Bun and cheese weekend is here, and I met the sexiest of men today." Suddenly, a frown creased her attractive medium-brown face as she gazed down at her flatmate.

"This morning you were all soca-frisky. What are you looking so 'blue' about now?"

"Just give me the bag of goodies and go wash for dinner," Carmen said.

"Come to think of it," Natasha said, dumping the bag into Carmen's arms," it is odd that there's no soca in this place."

"I'll explain my gloom over dinner," Carmen said, moving off to the tiny kitchen. Nothing could ever spoil Natasha's appetite. Natasha skipped across to the stereo on the other side of the little living-dining room and soon calypso filled the room.

Ten minutes later, the girls were seated at their smal' dining table over a thick vegetable and chicken soup. Both were in ripped jeans and T-shirt. The soca album on the stereo was turned down low. Natasha's head and shoulders jigged to the beat.

"I strongly suspect that my Zealous daddy has more than just a simple protest march up his wily sleeves," Carmen declared, "Perhaps something like a roadblock."

Natasha's head shot up from her soup and she put aside her spoon, which was remarkable because, like most tall and trim soca lovers, she was an avid eater - what, with all that crazy energetic soca-jumping-and-prancing about of hers, plus aerobic exercises, her tall lean body needed lots of calories, especially now that Carnival Week was at hand. "It'd be something if they should block the Sandy Gully bridge on Constant Spring Road," she breathed. "Goodness, it would mean ..."

"That's it!" Carmen exclaimed, cutting off Natasha's statement, and clutching her head, "That's it, I feel it in my bones. I can just see him and his council of elders giving their hundreds of followers a surprise order to block the bridge, and of course they'll do it with mindless obedience.

"I am willing to bet my future he hasn't told Mom the whole truth of his plan. Only his council of elders would know and be sworn to secrecy."

"Won't he be forced to withdraw if we publicized our suspicion?"

"No way," Carmen said, "He and his council would either simply take the no-comment stand, or lie."

"Lie publicly?" Natasha frowned. "Come on Carmen, you yourself say he's totally honest. So how could he lie in public? And saying 'no-comment' would be equal to saying yes he intends to have his followers block the bridge."

"My dear friend, he and his councillors wouldn't hesitate to lie, kill and plunder if they thought it was for the 'Glory of the Lord'. They are fanatics!" She grunted. "He once told my brothers and I that if he should ever turn from the church and the 'Spirit' told us to, we shouldn't hesitate to poison him, or blow out his brains with a gun.

"That's the type of zealots he and his councillors are!"

Natasha was stunned, "You never told me this before."

87

"Never told anyone before."

They fell silent, hearing but no longer aware of the soca music from the stereo. Neither one touched her soup.

"We must tell the carnival organisers our fears," Natasha finally broke the quiet.

"No," Carmen said thoughtfully, "That would cause confusion and boost Dad's fervour.

"Between us, and perhaps Pat, we must find a way to set him up for blackmail before the Road March day." She sighed. "At times like these I think we ought to double our efforts to find our dream husbands."

Later that Holy Thursday night, after a thunderous sermon at his Molynes-Road 'head tabernacle', Pastor Brown was telling his wife to "strip and kneel on the bed." They were in their dull, bleak but well lit bedroom. He was in his black 'holy gown' and flashing his 'holy belt' - the holy belt was a fat old leather belt, less its buckle, with 'holy words' carved on both sides.

Mrs. Brown was, as always, resigned to her flogging. She had stupidly allowed the devil, she mused, to lead her earlier that day to ask her husband to either call off the protest march, or set it for another day. What a sin! Why was she doubtful of what The Lord had instructed her husband to do? Wasn't the protest march a necessary good? Why did she continue to think it might ruin their church?

"My husband and master," Mrs. Brown said when she was naked, "I have sinned against you, our church and The Lord. Show me no mercy." She then went to turn on the tape-deck on the chest of drawers, flooding the room with gospel music. Next she kneeled on the bed, near the edge, her fleshy, brown bum high.

Feeling the usual rush of 'righteous excitement', Pastor Brown raised the holy belt. Before the first lash hit her flesh it occurred to Mrs. Brown that although she wouldn't be able to sit comfortably during the long Good Friday service tomorrow, tonight would be the first Holy Thursday night of fiery passion she had ever known. Her husband and herself were always strangely turned on after each flogging, she acknowledged.

She felt heat reach to her core at the same time as the first powerful lash. She grunted, feeling a heady mix of pain and pleasure, and before the

second lash descended she thought it might be fun to have regular floggings. It was a new and delicious thought.

Pastor brought down the holy belt on his wife's ample bum again
and again. All powerful lashes. After the fourth he lost count, his righteous excitement mounting with each lash, his hardness lurching under his gown at each of his wife's grunts and moans. He didn't - never
did - question his sexual excitement. He saw it as part of righteous love
and faithfulness towards his wife.

That same Thursday night, Harry's wife - asleep with one pillow
between her legs and one in her embrace - dreamed that she was flogging Harry with her new 'supple-jack' in front of hundreds of carnival
Road March fans in Kingston, the onlookers howling their delight,
urging her on. The lassoed Harry was on the ground writhing and
pleading, screaming with each lash, the coconut oil and oil-a-stay-ya in
which the 'supple-jack' had soaked for weeks causing the whip to glis-
ten in the sunlight. Smack! Scream. Delightful howls from onlookers.
Smack!

The dream switched to a banana field. The light was dusky. She
was still flogging Harry, but this time they were both naked and she
was using a leather strap. Harry's huge erection was aglow, waving
and lurching, as he twisted, rolled about, grovelling, a drunken grin
plastered on his face...

She awoke breathing heavily and began to laugh quietly. Fate was
going to lead her to Harry during the coming Road March. Harry
would soon be home where he belonged, and not as the master he was
before he ran away. She'd call the shots this time around.

Chapter 18

"But a whey yu dey whole day yesterday an' las' night Harry?" Mavis acosted Jenny's former man on the veranda of his tenement home in Kencot, Kingston. It was late Good Friday morning and Mavis was dressed in a long skirt, slippers and a male vest. "Rum an' loose woman in dis holy season." She said reproachfully.

"But Mavis, how yu so damn forward?" Snorted Natty, Mavis' children's father and common-law husband of many years. "De man no big man, older than you?"

"Lawd Natty, Harry not a touchy person."

Though not in the best of spirits after last evening's heavy drinking and some 'hard-work' at a go-go dancer's home, the dishevelled and bleary eyed Harry recognised that gleam in Mavis' eyes and sheen of her dark-brown face that said she had hot news he would love to hear.

Must be news of Jenny. Mavis never bothered to give men news unless it was news she was sure they would pay for if necessary.

"What a way fe greet a motherless an' womanless man pon dis day," Harry said with forced cheer.

"Sidung ya an' hear me out!" Mavis said, glowing, pushing Harry towards the chair next to Natty's. "News fe yu! A don't even tell Natty." Harry wasn't fooled, knowing Natty was always the last person to get Mavis' news. Akimbo before the two men, her eyes dramatically wide, Mavis bent forward and said "Me se' Jenny a go up Hope Road in a taxi yesterday, 'bout 3 o'clock!"

Natty kept a dead-pan face, his handsome black features giving away nothing. Harry nodded as if only moderately interested, but his heart was pounding and his ears buzzing for more specifics.

Well, one never needed to drag news out of Mavis.

"She no live a no Mobay," Mavis resumed, indignant that Jenny had lied to her. "She still dey a town ya! Dat's why she no write me. By her hairdo, new jewelry and expensive clothes yu can be sure say she tak' up wid one a dem uptown soca-man - 'member how she love de soca music an' carnival? How she did want fe ina carnival marchin'?"

Harry nodded. "Yu can sure a goin' serch fe har."

Natty fought back a chuckle. He suspected that Harry would be turning Carinval Week upside down looking for Jenny.

Mavis gave one of her gossipy hand-claps along with her usual accompanying. "Hey-hey!" Then: "Me sure say a some money man she gone to, for she not the type to whore."

"She might soon get a shock, doh. Money man always a tak' up ghetto girl, doll dem up an' den run dem out because him friend dem start to bad-mouth him 'bout him ghetto girl. Ghetto woman mus' stay wid har ghetto man an' together fight to better dem-selves. Like me an' Natty -- we soon buy a house uptown."

"Den Harry, yu woulda tak har back?"

"Jus' fe teach har a lesson," Harry said, getting to his feet. Mavis, he knew, had no more facts to give him. "Jus' fe teach har a lesson."

Jodi and Carl Azee, were enjoying Jodi's pool on Good Friday morning. They lived beside each other, near to the University of the West Indies, in the Mona Heights area of Kingston. Jodi's parents and fourteen year-old twin brothers were inside the two storey house. She had decided on a morning swim, and summoned Carl because she thought it was best to sweeten him up before her fiancé arrived from Negril that afternoon. Her fiancé would be staying at her house until Tuesday morning, so she wouldn't be able to give Carl any attention until then.

It was necessary to keep his lust piqued, and so she was in her skimpiest red bikini - she loved bright colours - which made her even-toned, yellowish-brown complexion even fairer. Carl was in ripped, cut-off jeans and muscle-vest. Sturdy and bronzed, his sole failing was an uncontrollable lust for Jodi. He had trembled with it for years, and Tuesday night's love-making had clinched his enslavement. He would kill for her, die for her. He had no further desire for the school girls he could have at any time. Blinding one or both of Jenny's eyes in the Road March was a small risk to take when the prize was more sex with Jodi. Perhaps he'd even win her away from that cur from Negril. He didn't care why Jodi wanted black Jenny blinded.

"Carl darling," Jodi, purred, her wet body perched on the rim of the front-yard pool, "my fiancé is coming this afternoon and will be here until Tuesday. Now, although I am seriously considering leaving him for you, I must be dedicated to him because Mom and Dad invited him. It wouldn't do to let them feel bad." She sighed, her bosom heaving. Carl took a deep breath. "It was they who caused us to be engaged in the first place.

Anyway, after Tuesday you and I will enjoy the best part of Carnival. Then after you have proved your love during the Road March I'll be all yours to love as much as you want."

"The black bitch Jenny is already blind," Carl said with quiet passion from his seat . "I won't fail you my dove. Then I'll show you why I am the right man for you."

"Blind the bitch for hitting me, and anything is possible."

"You mean she dared to hit you!"

"With a stick," Jodi lied with false grief and embarrassment. "And you know ghetto girls are used to fighting."

"Why not let me fix Dave as well?" He was ready to slay Dave.

"No," Jodi said. "God will fix him in time. Just blind one of the black bitch's eyes. Dave never hit me but she did."

"I'll fix her during the Road March."

"We'll spend the whole night at a motel."

"I can't wait," he breathed, losing himself in her glittering eyes and smile. God, how beautiful she was, the only perfect woman.

"Neither can I." She moved her eyes down to his pants front. "I keep dreaming of your hands and tongue," - she squirmed dramatically "and your strong... thing."

He shuddered with desire, his hardness painful. "Jodi can't we have some sex before the Road March, please darling?"

Jodi pouted prettily. " I told you already. You have too wild a reputation. And every man wants my body. You must prove yourself first." She smiled sweetly and stood, stretching her sexy body slowly, provocatively. "I can tell you, I won't be giving my silly fiancé any sex while he's here." She moistened her lips enticingly. "So I will be all fresh and oh so tight for you on Road March night." She winked and dived into the pool.

Carl was breathing heavily, aching for her, ready to fake the accident by which he'd blind one of Jenny's eyes. Road March come quick, he prayed, come fast.

Chapter 19

*L*ike most Jamaicans, Jenny and Dave were chronically late for Good Friday service. Jenny wasn't aware that Mavis had seen her yesterday evening. They would have skipped the long Good Friday service and attended the Easter one on Sunday evening or morning, but Carnival Week was going to kick off Sunday, at Chukka Cove, on the island's North Coast. They, instead decided they would sleep late Sunday morning to rest up for the bumpy 40 mile drive and the ensuing nine to ten hour jump-up soca fete.

Dave's parents along with the parents of Bette and her 'Troopers' were present when he and Jenny made their late entrance to one of the city's top Anglican churches. It was a full house. Some ten minutes later, the elegantly dressed Bette and her equally elegant 'Troopers' slipped into the back pew with sly smirks.

Jenny felt a bit awed by the majestic old stone church and by the solemn air of the Anglican service. Formerly, whenever she did go to church it was to a Baptist one. Her mother had been a half-hearted Baptist who circled all the city's Baptist churches. But Jenny didn't feel out of place. Her new off-white silk dress, mantilla and sheer stockings were of as fine a quality as any in that elegant crowd, and Dave was the handsomest of the men. He made his grey suit seem priceless. She had tried to talk him out of buying her such expensive things, but she was now glad he had sternly insisted on buying her the best.

Jenny sensed eyes boring into her back. She snuck a look behind her to meet the snotty smiles of Bette, Anette and Joan and a hostile glower from Dorret, who were a few pews behind her and Dave.

Was there no getting rid of that bunch of freaks? mused Jenny, and it seemed as if Dorret was becoming more and more hostile towards her. They always looked so lovely but that only belied how evil they were. At least she wouldn't meet Jodi here. Jodi and her family were Catholics.

Dave thought Jenny seemed a bit nervous in the unfamiliar surroundings. He took her hand and squeezed it reassuringly as they rose for a hymn. He was sure that every man and woman present knew Jenny was the most beautiful lady in this attractive crowd.

Seeing Dave's intimate squeeze of Jenny's hand, and that sweet smile of his, Dorret almost crushed her hymnal. Her stomach churned bitterly with jealous rage, and she was unable to join the lofty start of the hymn. The piping of the organ grated on her nerves. How she hated that black bitch Jenny. She should have declared her love to Dave soon after he and Jodi had broken up.

With an inward sigh Dorret forced herself to join in song, thinking that once she seduced Dave next week Saturday he would awaken from the sordid spell which Jenny had cast. He would then get rid of Jenny.

Singing lustily, Bette was aware of Dorret's discomfort and the cause of it. How could Dave overlook a girl like Dorret and be smitten with Jenny? Granted, Jenny was pretty and had a certain charm and was well-spoken, but she was barely educated and from the ghetto and black, Dorret's colour and back-ground on the other hand were similar to Dave's, even though Dorret wouldn't be able to match his inheritance.

But Dor was a bright career lady who earned good money and was destined for the very top of the corporate ladder.

Men, Bette thought, singing along lustily, men were so unpredictable — white, brown, black. Hadn't her British uncle married a penniless half-mad German whore?

At the end of the church service, Jenny had to endure being introduced around by Dave's parents. There were a few disapproving frowns as word about her background had already spread, but for the most part Jenny was warmly greeted. The males (from lads to grandfathers) were all delighted to meet Jenny. They all thought her unlike their idea of ghetto people and either damn sexy or 'lovely-though-black'. Nobody asked or said anything embarrassing, since they knew Dave and his father weren't men to trifle with, and it was obvious that Dave's parents liked Jenny.

Glowing with happiness, Jenny and Dave stopped on the short drive home to eat the bun and cheese they had packed before leaving home.

"How wonderful it would be if bun and cheese was as sweet as you, my love," Dave said passionately, "as tasty as your two lips."

"How naughty of you!" Jenny forced a frown, "Just coming from church too!" She said with mock seriousness. Swallowing a bit of cheese she added, "All the same, I do wish there was something half as delicious," her eyes moved down to his lap, "as the refreshingly sweet juice that I enjoy when I milk a certain organ."

They grinned at each other, eyes locked in devilish conspiracy as they slowly chewed bun and cheese.

I must propose to her soon or die, he thought. She was made for me.

She was thinking the same thing.

Chapter 20

Over the past few weeks, the coming Carnival Week, especially the Road March, was the main topic of discussion all across the island. Before 1990, Carnival was something most Jamaicans only heard and read about as happening in Trinidad while glimpsing snatches of it on television; and participating and visiting Trinidad was reserved only for the uptown browning. Now that Carnival had reached Jamaica, it was bitterly decried by church leaders. Heated arguments, for and against it were being tossed back and forth with great passion and equally varied opinions emanating from various quarters of society.

Six youngmen were seated on a scarred fence in an east Kingston ghetto on Good Friday evening. Three were smoking marijuana, two of whom were dreadlocks. They were discussing carnival.

"Me can't wait fe de Road March me idrens," said one of the 'comb-heads'. "It sweet me fe see de uptown girls dem whinin' up half naked. De fuckin' greatest show pon earth! Dem uptown 'brownings' really get off pon soca!"

"Me glad sey more woman dan man in it!"

"It really nice fe see de stoosh girls a go-on like go-go in the streets," said the smoking 'comb-head'. "Me recognise two browning beauty queen las' year a go-on worse dan go-go."

"De idrens know de browning teller out at Barclay Bank who always a skin-up har nose pon ghetto idren?" asked one of the dreadlocks. "Man yu shoulda did see har!"

"Me love when two, three or four a de gals dem a whine up in a train."

"Only de Road March interest me. A woulda swim pon dry land an' walk pon sea fe see it. De ladies truly look nice and fit, brownings and blacks an' white alike. Mek' yu proud to be Jamaican. De I dem 'member say, if I sick pon dat day unnu mus' carry I out pon a stretcher!"

"Fuckin' sexiest show pon earth!"

"Yes I, sexier dan any sex show!"

A group of four ghetto girls in a drab room in downtown Kingston that same evening were eating bun and cheese.

"De only reason I wouldn't dance in carnival Road March is 'cause woman out-number man by too much. Is like all de man dem want to just stand an' lust pon woman."

"True. Nothin' wrong with it fe true except de absence of male dancers. Dat mak' it look as if woman a show-piece or 'poppy-show'."

"Las' year me had was fe crane me neck like hell fe se' de few hairy chest and bulgin' legs."

"Me coulda even glimpse one heavy front!"

Laughter.

"No, because man so few de girls dem always surround dem."

"It sure did hurt me how me man him jus' a look an' grin so while me coulda hardly see anythin' fe excite me. A did mad fe start fight him right dey!"

More laughter.

"An' to t'ink de uptown gal dem suppose to be more liberated dan we?"

"Dem jus' love show off dem self without havin' to tak' a good fuck."

"Lawd! Elvin nearly kill me fe de whole week after las' year Road March!"

"Down to de dead rise dat Sunday evening an' night!"

Howling laughter.

"So carnival is just over a day away," said the soca-loving ultra-feminist, single, professional young lady to her two flat-mates as she nibbled bun and cheese in the colourful living-dining room of their fifth storey, three bedroom apartment in the Kingston ten area.

"Bigger and better this year they claim," stated the other lady. "So next week Sunday, sorry; I mean week after next Sunday, we shall see hundreds of our sisters - including so many of the so-called liberated ones - all cheapening womanhood."

"Most girls only pay lip service to being progressive," commented the man. "That's why you girls shouldn't put the blame all on me when I change girls so often."

"We do understand, sort of, anyway. But just as we are single and don't sleep around, you shouldn't either."

"Plus what would we do without our protector, life-long friend and sounding-board? Can't afford to lose you to AIDS!"

"You won't," he said.

"Back to the Road March," said one of the ladies. "Surely the sisters should insist on a quota. Even say 40% men; in which case I would gladly take part."

"Our women still are far from being liberated. Still mental slaves."

Saturday morning three brown middle-aged men, a brown young-man, two young brown girls and a black middle-aged woman were seated on a veranda in a middle-class Kingston neighbourhood.

All were avid music fans.

"I telling you people," the young man was explaining, "that many soca artists are stealing old reggae ideas. I hear they are trying DJ stuff, just as Black Americans copied our DJs while saying Rap is one hundred percent American. Soca train and line dancing stuff are based on the early eighties reggae 'every-posse-form-a-line' craze.

"And now this grab-something-and-wave soca business. Again in the early eighties our DJs had a 'waving' craze: you couldn't go to a dance without having to wave-off your hand. And we have been bubbling since the seventies.

"Then there are the soca hits which are nothing but remakes of old reggae hits, like 'Chalice In The Palace' and 'Dubbing It To Your Majesty'."

"Are you saying that soca and carnival are plots or threat against reggae music?" asked one of the young ladies.

"No," the young-men replied evenly. "Reggae is global these days. Anywhere in the world you go, people hold the names Bob Marley and Reggae in reverence. Calypso is much older than reggae but not half as successful. And soca is calypso, regardless of what you want to say; just as dancehall is reggae.

Marley drew crowds of over seventy to eighty thousand in places such as Rome; and no five or six soca artistes' estate put together is worth half as much as Marley's. In fact, reggae is no longer purely a Jamaican product as you have many British, American and Asian reggae acts of all colour. Plus reggae is now mixed with Rap and Rock. Next, I predict, you'll be seeing the US and European mega-stars cutting albums with top reggae acts.

My grouse with carnival is that you can't have a 'Jamaican Carnival' and not use at least 33% reggae. Of course, reggae can't fit into the road march. But the shows should be using a soca/reggae mix."

"So you intend to go to the reggae show Monday night instead of a carnival fete?" asked the young-man's girl with a pout.

"No," the young-man responded, a smile on his brown face. "You and I shall be at the soca show at the Institute because I have seen the reggae artists over and over; secondly, Easter weekend was never a reggae stage show time. Easter Holiday was always beach and dancehall. So no reggae promoter should try to out-do carnival. Carnival is a good idea. It gives the people a wider scope of entertainment and can attract lots of tourist for the road march and last fetes. But I still feel that the stage shows and fetes, should offer some reggae to give it a truly Jamaican stamp. Such a unique show would be bound to attract more tourists. What we had last year and will be having this year is only a copy of the Eastern Caribbean carnivals."

At noon, a quadroon mother entered her 19 year-old daughter's bedroom with a gloomy face. The daughter was 'whiter' than her mother because the daughter's father was white. They lived in a mansion in Mona Heights and were Anglicans.

"Darling dearest," the mother said, "I have come to again beg you not to dance in that barbaric carnival Road March. Soca music is nice - far better then the gutter stuff called reggae - but all those blacks staring at your half naked body in the street. Just the thought gets me down."

"Mom. You are twenty-five percent black!"

The mother flushed angrily. She didn't like being reminded of her black quarter, which wasn't that prominent due to her bleached skin, constant hiding from the sun and her naturally tawny brown hair and light-coloured eyes. Anyway, she now fought down her anger as she sat down on one of the quilted bedroom chairs and crisply said "You, at least, have very little claim to kin with blacks. So you shouldn't be wanting to act like a go-go dancer in the streets with thousands of them staring."

The daughter sat up in the middle of her huge bed and sighed, "I am proud of my negro blood. Not that I'd prefer if I were a mulatto or black. But one can't help marvelling at the physical and spiritual strength it took blacks to survive the most savage slave system of all times. The European race would have disappeared under similar circumstances. See, our black ancestors have something over our white ones."

"The problem," the mother bristled, "is that your father failed to be firm with you! But tell me, is it Christian-like to dance half-naked in the streets on a Sunday?"

"Mom! I won't be half-naked, I am an adult and not a real Christian! And carnival is sensual not vulgar. Besides, lusting men are all the same — black, white or brown."

Saturday at noon saw five farmers in a hut at the top of a hillside banana/plantain/yam field in Portland venting their own sentiments about carnival. Two of the three middle-aged farmers were Pentecostal Christians, the other was a Methodist. The rest were non-religious.

"So de devil carnival come again," said one of the middle-aged farmers. "Why dem hav' to keep de Road March pon a Sunday?"

"More curse pon de land," said another of the middle-aged farmers.

"De devil work! In Trinidad an' dem places dem don't keep it Sunday day."

"T'ing is," one of the young farmers explained, "in Trinidad an' dem other islands carnival is mainly a government run t'ing. So de whole nation support it an' close down for de weekday Road March. Here, carnival - Byron Lee's an' de others - is a private business.

"Question is, will de government an' Jamdown people agree to give up a week-day for de Road March? Remember, if dem move it to Saturday de Adventists goin' mek' noise."

"Daddy, on which other day could the Road March be kept?" A seventeen year-old girl was imploring in Spanish Town. She and her father were on the back veranda of their middle-class home. "Move the Kiddies Carnival to Friday and put Road March on Saturday and you'd have the adventists and lots of business-men screaming murder. Perhaps after a while Jamaicans will be so used to carnival that it would be possible to have the Road March on a week-day but for now Sunday is the only suitable day."

One dreadlocks and one 'comb-head' were seated on the border of their marijuana fields in Westmoreland later that evening.

"So de church man dem an' de soca people look like dem woulda love to knock fist over carnival Road March," commented the comb-head planter.

"Good," said the dreadlocks. "Babylon divided, more power to I an' I an' less trouble from cops."

"So what reggae show Monday night?" One youth in a West Kingston ghetto asked his friend. It was late Saturday night and they were returning from a dance.

"No iya," came the prompt reply. "Easter Monday was never a reggae show time. Why dem promoter want fe knock 'gainst de carnival. We gettin' a free Road March so we no mus' try fe support de payin' shows?

"I a go a one a de soca jams early Monday night, den hit a dancehall. Easter Monday was always nuff dancehall but not reggae stage shows."

"Me hear nuff man a sey de same t'ing iya. Both who hav' an' who no hav' money. Plus man see all de reggae acts set fe Monday nuff time but never see de soca acts."

"Is justice iya. Everyt'ing mus' hav' it time an' place. We hav' de whole year fe reggae shows, an' we have Reggae Sunsplash, so why run 'gainst de carnival?"

"Plus no live reggae show cyan sweet like when yu put four singer an' four DJ live in a dancehall mek' dem come down live-an'-direct pon de dub plates!"

"True sounds, iya man, true sounds."

"Instead a ' hurry-come-up' reggae show, de promoter shoulda did put on a show featurin' old reggae acts and old calypso acts."

"Blo-wow! Dat a one champion idea! Man like U-Roy, I-Roy, John Holt, Sparrow an' some more older calypso acts inna one show."

"Woulda offer a good choice to dose who don't like de jump-up soca shows."

"Man, a tell yu, we ghetto-ites only want a way fe get cash fe back dem kinda idea. We always havin' some good idea, but how fe get dem up-front wid-out cash?"

"Anyway, I intend fe go jammin' to some soca fo' a change."

Section Three:

Earth's Sexiest and Merriest Show!

Chapter 21

Uh—huh !
The right one!
Here comes the big one baby! Aw ah!
Big whining! Huge dip! Round the world!
Uh-huhh! Aw-ahh! Oh-oh for earth's merriest-and-sexiest Show! mi-huh
uh-huh aw-ah!

Easter Sunday, last day of March 1991, dawned with a bang. People flocked to the morning church services in their best attire. Many hadn't been to church since either Christmas or last Easter. All literally smelled of the bun and cheese they had been gorging on since Holy Thursday. There were many Easter sermons against the carnival Road March set for next week and much support for Pastor Brown's protest march.

Many carnivalites, too, went to morning service. But others, like Dave and Jenny, Bette her three 'Troopers' and Jodi, thought it best to sleep late and get some extra rest for the giant show which was to kick off the major carnival at four on the enchanting North coast of the island. The other smaller carnivals set for Carnival Week were also to begin that day with several fetes in Kingston and the Western end of the island.

Easter services at the island's eight Zealous Pentecostal temples saw Pastor/Bishop Brown and other church leaders imploring one and all to be early for the protest march next Sunday.

Pastor Brown's wife was no longer distressed over the protest march. In fact, since Thursday night's 'holy flogging' and the ensuing wild love-making her major concern had been to find a way to get Pastor to use his holy-belt more often without her seeming too wanton a woman. Should she simply tell him how much she liked the passion he showed after each flogging? That she had actually enjoyed this last flogging? But hadn't her reactions, especially this last time, showed him how she felt? Why hadn't she seen this highly erotic side before?

Anyway, coming out with it bluntly might not be wise. It could make her seem like a whore.

Now, seated in the choir's pews listening to her husband's thunderous Easter sermon, dressed in dark-blue and safe behind a black veil, Mrs. Brown squirmed to ease the slight discomfort of her bum, which was still a bit sore from Thursday's flogging and the two wild rides that had followed. Sitting through the long Good Friday service had been worse but far less uncomfortable then she had expected; in addition to several fake trips to the bathroom, she had, safe behind her veil, called up memories of the nights' sweet passion to drown out the discomfort of her seat. Now she willed aside the sensual thoughts at the edge of her mind, and gave her full attention to her husband's Easter sermon.

Carmen Brown went to a Baptist church with her flat-mate Natasha. Not that either of them saw themselves as Christians, but like most Jamaicans, they thought it was decent to go to church at Easter. Natasha had grown up in a Baptist family so they attended the nearest Baptist church since Carmen refused to set foot in a church of her father's faith.

Carmen and Natasha gave much thought to the subject at hand but hadn't come up with a plan to coerce Pastor Brown into calling off his protest march. This Easter afternoon however a promising plan began to take shape in Carmen's mind as she and Natasha with a friend and her husband were travelling out to Chukka Cove for the North coast's carnival opening. Carmen, dressed in a colourful pants-suit, leaned back in the Toyota with a contented grin as the plan grew in her mind. She peeped across at Natasha, who was dolled up as a dashing pirate and looking out the window. Tomorrow, Carmen thought, tomorrow I shall put this daring plan to Natasha.

Jodi was in high spirits, her make-up, a thick colourful mask. She looked like one of the fairy princess that she still liked to read about. She was in her 'little red dress', strapped in beside her somber fiancé as he sped them towards the North coast. Jodi was thinking about last night's passion. Her fiancé had spent most of the night in her bed before sneaking back to the guest room. Of course, her parents knew she had lost her virginity long ago and that she slept with her fiancé, but they were Catholics. Appearances were important.

Jodi's thoughts suddenly switched to Dave: Her fiancé was as good a lover as Dave was, she thought, better in some ways in fact, and richer and whiter and easier to control... But... but Dave was so much more interesting. Her fiancé was so dull out of bed.

Jodi glanced across at her fiancé's handsome but inanimate features and her spirits sank. He was so damn boring out of bed... If that black bitch... well Carl was going to fix the black slut in the Road March, just seven more days. After that, Dave would beg her to come back to him.

She imagined Dave kneeling and pleading with teary eyes, "Jodi come back! Jodi my love! Come back to me!"

And she'd take him back, Jodi mused, take him back and get rid of her socially inept fiancé. And, of course, Dave's affair with Jenny would be the whip with which she'd keep him slaving to please her for life.

Black slut Jenny, Jodi smiled to herself, perhaps you are a blessing after all. Maybe someday I will even pay you for providing me with a handle over Dave's blade.

Dave's car was in the middle of a long line of traffic bound for the North coast. Seated beside him, Jenny was a beautiful picture in a white mini cut-work dress, silver stockings, matching shoes and jewelry, her bright make-up, tastefully applied. Dave thought she was about the closest one could get in resemblance to the legendary Queen of Sheba — said by King Solomon to have been the loveliest beauty of all time. Dave was in broad-striped green/blue pants and shirt. He recognised Bette's BMW several cars ahead as the long line of vehicles twisted through the Bog Walk gorge. Dave had always loved the tranquility of this area and the seeming laziness of the Rio Cobre River; they approached Flat Bridge which would take them from one side of the river to the other and his throughts moved back to the fun time ahead.

Bette and her three 'Troopers' were lounging in the back of the car being chauffeur-driven by their two smiling young brown male escorts. The one at the wheel was just nineteen but a very good driver. The ladies were in brand-new, green jeans, pink sleeve-less silk blouses, white socks and canvas shoes. Laced through their hair were bright ribbons and feathers, their faces and nails streaked with a motley design of colour. In short, these ladies were decked out just right for ranting, raving and misbehaving.

Carnival fans had turned out in droves for the North coast's beach-side calypso/soca, carnival opening. Most were middle-class and had driven in from Kingston and Montego Bay, the island's second city in the West. But there were cars from every parish. The luscious well laid out grounds of the sport resort were ideal for a carnival jump-up. The bright Sunday afternoon was cooled by salty fragrant winds rolling gently off the emerald sea.

By half past four things were already hot, hot, hot, as the revellers jumped, 'waved-something' and 'dollar-whined', and gyrated to the blood-pumping, spine-tingling, nonstop soca music. It was mainly outdoor live music, featuring two of the very best soca bands - Byron Lee from Jamaica, the Renegades from Trinidad - and five of the Eastern Caribbean's best soca names artistes. There was also recorded music by Andrew Henry's - Renegades, one of the island's few soca discos. The well stocked bars and food stalls were doing a brisk business.

By dusk couples were sneaking off — some staggering drunkenly — to remote sections of the huge grounds and beach for hotter action.

Dave was doing his best to steer clear of Bette and her three Troops. He didn't see Jodi as any threat to Jenny's happiness. After all, Jodi was with her fiancé. Bette and her Troops were the only ones who could spoil Jenny's immense glee tonight, Dave thought.

It was just after seven o'clock, under a starry sky, before Bette and company finally ran Dave and Jenny to earth by one of the bars. Bette and her 'Troopers' were tipsy, not being used to hard liquor. Bette drunkenly demanded that Dave dance with her. Dave seeing no way out, led her from the well-lighted bar area after asking his friend Joe to look after Jenny.

Sipping a beer laced with rum, Dorret was glowering at Jenny.

Ignoring Dorret, Jenny wasn't amused by Bette forcing Dave to the dance area by the bandstand. To make matters worse one of Jenny's favourite soca hits — by that breathtakingly beautiful Trinidadian Carnival Queen

— was next, and Anette immediately slurred in Jenny's ear "Jenniee is it true... tru you an' Daviee goot engaged?"

"No," Jenny responded crisply, her indignation soaring, "Too early for that."

"Well I hope you'll be... around lo..long eenough fo'.." Anette was slurring when Joe, sensing that trouble was brewing, whisked Jenny away for an energetic bout of dancing which soon had Jenny sweating, laughing and shouting with those around them.

Joe's girlfriend was quite comfortable at a table with her twin sister. The alcohol had come near to causing Anette to shout her contempt after Joe and Jenny but she checked her heavy tongue in time.

Afterwards, Bette, Anette, then Dorret followed by Joan took short turns dancing with Dave. Alcohol had always made Dorret somewhat coolly detached, now she was far too hammered to be sentimental about dancing with Dave. All she could think of was seducing him in the near future.

Jenny had no time to brood. After several dances with Joe she found herself literally snatched away from him by his teenaged brother and several other teenaged boys. The energetic youngsters obviously got a great kick out of dancing with 'Dave's girl', just as they had gotten a great kick out of tiring out Joe's half-Chinese-half-white girl and her twin. Jenny was dripping sweat and thinking about a chair by the time Dave was able to rescue her from the boys.

"Go seek your size!" Dave admonished teasingly to the grinning boys.

"Actually," Jenny teased, "they are better dancers than you and Joe."

"See!" The boys exclaimed before running off after a colourful group of teenaged girls.

Each time she glimpsed Jenny and Dave, Jodi felt a stab of jealous anger. Her fiancé was such a poor dancer compared to Dave. She had to call off her engagement and get Dave to return to her. Dave was fun in and out of bed, an excellent dancer and talker and he knew about every sport there was.

Well, Jodi mused, thank God her plan would be carried out soon. Then getting back Dave would be very easy.

At about 10 o'clock, just as the silvery half moon was coming over the sea's dark horizon the sensual atmosphere overwhelmed Jenny and Dave.

With two bottles of very cold Red Stripe beers, they headed for a private area of the sprawling grounds.

Jodi, dancing with her fiancé, saw Jenny and Dave sneaking off and knew what was about to happen. Seething with jealousy, Jodi mistakenly kneed her fiancé in his groin. He doubled over there in the crowd of dancing couples, clutching his front and gasping like a fish out of water. Jodi felt a strong urge to land him a few more kicks for good measure. Oh how she was getting to hate the bastard. How could she have up to this day thought he was the ideal husband?

Still, Jodi controlled her disgust and feigned the concern she knew onlookers expected of her.

A drunk old American doctor examined Jodi's groaning fiancé and declared "All is well... hic... later t'night you'll be... hic.. humpin'... hic her harder than...hic ever."

While this little melodrama was going on. Carl Azee was at the Oakridge soca party in Kingston wishing he was with Jodi at Chukka Cove and thinking about his resolution to blind one of Jenny's eyes to please Jodi.

Dancing with a seventeen year-old , near-white, school-girl, Carl conjured up images of Jodi, dressed in his favourite colours, red and black, dancing her special sensual dance. Then he pictured her naked and dancing.

He'd do anything to please Jodi and to be her lover. He'd commit a string of murders if that's what it took.

He had no qualms about wounding Dave's nobody black girlfriend as long as it'd make it possible for him to become Jodi's husband!

The girl Carl was dancing with placed her hands on his shoulders and jutted her pelvis forward.

Carl met her pelvic thrusts. This little bitch is hot for it, he thought. He had had her a few times already. Tonight he was going to show her that fucking can hurt her. He was going to ravish and maul her, she wasn't Jodi. He despised her, hated all girls but Jodi. Why the fuck couldn't this bitch and all the others be even half as beautiful and sweet and good in bed as Jodi?

Was there ever another girl, and will there ever be another, as beautiful as Jodi?

Chapter 22

Mr. and Mrs. Hurt spent the Easter evening with their boys watching TV. Mrs. Hurt was pondering her lover's desire for her to leave her husband and marry him. Her body and heart wanted her to go. But the voice of reason made her hesitate - could she bear to break with her Catholic faith and risk losing her rotten sons?

But she had to tell Cedric her decision by weekend. What...?

Sitting there in the semi-dark television room, Mr. Hurt was thinking of Jenny's shapely thighs and lovely figure in tight gym-wear, wondering if she would ever seek to get closer to him. He had confirmed that she was indeed from the ghetto. He knew it was dangerous to get involved, but just couldn't get her out of his mind, no matter how hard he tried. Neither was he able to resist going to the Fit Centre just to see and exchange casual talk with her. She was invading his dreams. Her lovely black skin, her pretty face, her glorious legs!

What could he do to get her, Mr Hurt mused, without risking a confrontation with the gunmen...? Would it be possible, even though she didn't seem the least interested in two-timing her boyfriend? But he must have her, there must be a way.

Inspector Hinds and his wife went to a soca show in Kingston that Easter night. He had managed to talk his wife out of the North coast opening, promising her in the process, a new neck-lace and a week of her favourite sex game (him in bondage, which was at the bottom rung of his sexual favourite) after Carnival week.

The Inspector was in no mood for a trip out of the city, was in no mood for carnival, and didn't want to tell his wife about the rumours he had heard about Don J's plans for the day of the Road March. He hadn't learned anything further of the intended Road March kidnapping.

It was odd that the press and other cops hadn't yet heard anything of Don J's plans. If Paula knew, why not many others? Had Don J aimed the rumour at Paula specifically with the knowledge that she'd relay it to him and no one else? Or was Paula working with Don J?

The Inspector sat brooding in the midst of the shouting, and soca dancing in the Constant Spring Road plaza while his scantily clad wife ranted and raved all over the asphalted plaza with a string of panting men. He had to out-smart Don J. Had to win this case to ease some of his guilt over his corruption.

"Natasha," Carmen said over coffee at eleven the next morning at their dining table, "I have an idea which will force Dad to call off his devious protest march. It came to me last evening on the way to carnival. You'll be called upon to do a big part though."

"I am willing," Natasha said. She looked as beat as Carmen did. They were both still in night gowns having awoken not long ago. It had been near four o'clock that morning when their friends had seen them safely to their door after the drive back from last night's 'blowout'. Today was a public holiday, Easter Monday.

"What we'll do is this," Carmen explained, suddenly looking brighter. "I am going to have the Zealous Beast come here one day this week and put on a weepy show about wanting to return to his fold. Then I shall feed him a drink laced with Spanish Fly and a Downer or two. Then when he gets groggy we will take pictures of you and him in bed.

But we'll have to do it before noon so he can sleep off the drugs before night. Well?"

"It's a thrilling plan!" She high-fived Carmen. "I will enjoy posing with Bishop Brown. A great pity you won't allow me to do more than pose with him!"

They laughed.

Bette and her 'Troopers' had been dead drunk on the return trip from the north coast. Of all the girls parents, Dorret's mother had been the most distressed, seeing her giggling daughter being lifted inside by two young men at three in the morning.

Bette surfaced at noon feeling as stiff as a piece of board and thirsty. Her mouth tasted horrible. After a bath and shower and plenty black coffee she felt much better, and was able to subdue her parents' anger over her coming home drunk. She then phoned up her three Troops to tell each she'd soon be coming to cart them off to the Endurance Health Club.

"Exercise will get out last night's poison and make us fit for the Institute tonight," Bette told each girl over the phone. And although Joan and Anette had headaches they didn't demur.

Dressed in black body stockings, black gym top and a white sweatshirt, Bette drove to each of her 'Troopers' homes in the early afternoon. By then Joan and Anette had shaken off their headaches. The Monday afternoon was hot, which pleased Bette. Sweating was good after a night such as last night, she reasoned.

"We sure went overboard last night," Bette declared when she had picked up the last of her slouching, baggy-eyed Troopers. "It was opening night so perhaps getting drunk was apt. But it mustn't happen again before the last night of carnival. We must be fit for the Road March if our cell is to come out on top."

"I never want to get drunk again," Dorret groaned. She looked pink as a shrimp, and was in a three piece red and white gym-wear. "I don't recall getting home. Now I feel so weak and foul."

"The guys had to lift you inside," Bette said,. "That much I recall."

"My dad has been howling with laughter since I got up," Anette groaned. She was in shorts and tank top. Her face was pallid.

"Mine wasn't amused," Joan said, "though he didn't make a fuss like mom." She was in a multi-coloured one piece gym-wear. Her face seemed to be in danger of crumpling under the thick coat of hastily applied make-up.

Dorret thought it best not to share how her dad had commented that at last she had showed some human feelings.

At the Endurance Club, Bette had to goad herself and her 'Troopers' into beginning some exercise. But after fifteen minutes of sweating to light aerobics they began to feel stronger. They did a half hour of aerobics and floor exercises, then had a brief swim in the club's pool. Next they sat down to a late lunch at the club's cafe.

After nearly half hour with the rowing machine and weights, Bette and her 'Troopers' retired to the back-yard. They sat under a cherry tree watching some teens at a game of mixed doubles on the nearest of the three tennis courts.

"Bette and her gang," hailed the sturdily built young lady approaching them. She was in her early thirties, a dentist and a serious body builder. Her name was Donna, but in certain circles she was called 'Donald'.

Donna was brown, of medium height, broad shouldered and muscular with small breasts. She was a shameless lesbian. Today she was clad in a white one piece bathing suit over sheer black tights. "Just taking a rest," she explained, "and decided to come see if any of you girls have had a change of heart and were willing to move into my apartment."

"Still haven't found a new lady love?" Bette asked. To her, lesbians were an amusing set.

"Nope," Donna said with a sigh, sitting down beside Dorret. She had always had a strong feeling that Dorret was the only one of these girls who was susceptible to her charms and she loved Dorret's looks. "Want to try me, anyone of you. Just one night and you won't want to leave."

"Not my cup of tea dear," Bette smiled.

"What about you others?" Donna queried, her eyes coming to rest on Dorret.

Joan and Anette tolerated Donna because Bette treated her as a friend. Dorret was divided where Donna was concerned — lesbianism was anti-social, therefore she could never be lesbian or bisexual. But at times she found herself admiring Donna's body and she did see Donna as a friend. There were times when she wondered what it would be like to be in bed with her, though her attraction for Donna wasn't half as intense as the lust she had felt for her favourite junior high school teacher.

Now, Donna was gazing at her with open lust, so Dorret gave her usual answer: "If I am still unmarried at forty you can have me then."

"It will be a long wait sugar pie," Donna smiled, "but it will be worth it. Just you stay trim. In the meantime perhaps Joan and/or Anette would like to oblige?"

114

"Had my les phase long ago," Anette said. "Want no imitation. Only men can fill me with sweetness."

"Not interested," Joan said crisply.

Seeing that the others were paying keen attention to the tennis courts, Donna impulsively reached a hand to caress Dorret's bum. Dorret felt a bolt of electricity, her eyes met Donna's. Dorret blushed and moved away from Donna's hand.

I am not a lesbian, Dorret told herself, I love Dave and doctors say we all have homosexual phases. Donna is truly a nice friend, so witty, and our names are close.

Donna hadn't persisted in caressing Dorret. She kept her hand in check. Her heart pounded with love and lust. She was now sure she could seduce Dorret. I must somehow find ways, Donna thought, to get her away from these friends of hers.

"I wasn't able to make it to the Chukka Cove show last night," Donna said, forcing her tone to sound light. "I suppose you girls went?"

"Yea, and got roaring drunk!" Bette laughed.

"I don't believe it!" Donna exclaimed sincerely. "You girls drunk? All four of you?

"All four," Bette giggled. "Luckily we had two men to drive. It was wild!"

"Whatever caused you girls to go overboard?" Donna asked incredulously. "A mean you are supposed to be near as zealous as I am where health is concerned. Isn't hard alcohol on your hate list? I myself do take a beer now and then, of course."

"A beer or two is usually our limit," Bette conceded. "But the whole atmosphere last evening seemed super-charged. By dusk each of us had surpassed our two beer limit, each beer having a shot of rum! Oh, then there was no stopping us. Stronger and stronger drinks."

"Dancing to soca out in the open there at the seaside made it harder to get drunk," Joan sighed. "Half the amount of drinking at a party here would see us knocked out."

"Never shall I drink so much again," Anette vowed.

"Dorret, how drunk did you get?" asked Donna.

"Embarrassingly so," Dorret blushed. Her blush was due to more han the memory of the previous night's debauchery. She looked off beore adding "I don't remember half of what happened."

"The guys had to lift her out of the car to her bed," Bette laughed.

"Good grief," Donna chuckled in her manish-manner. But she felt a stab of jealousy inside at the thought of two men lifting Dorret. "I wish I was there."

Dorret felt strangely embarrassed.

"Never again will I get so sloshed," Bette declared.

After a few moments of silence Donna said " I haven't seen Dave for quite a while. Is he still with his black girl? I did hear he's now at the Fit Centre gym."

"They are as close as a letter and a stamp," Bette commented. "Saw them last night."

She shook her head. "I'd expected he'd have tired of her by this. But it seems even his parents have fallen for her."

Dorret had to fight to keep herself from scowling at Bette and she hoped none of her three closest friends dared to tell Donna of her interest in Dave.

"It truly is an odd happening," Donna said thoughtfully. One can understand him breaking off with silly feather-brained Jodi. But to take up with a ghetto girl who I hear is barely educated?"

"She told us so herself," Joan said. "One Sunday we paid them a surprise visit. She is a strange girl," Bette commented . "Actually she is well-spoken and bright, definitely brighter than Jodi."

"Few persons are as dumb as Jodi," Donna commented.

"But Jodi's so beautiful," Anette said to Donna. "Ever tried your hand at her?"

"I am not the type to sleep about and don't fancy girls who do," Donna responded evenly. "I love sex to be part of heart-felt love. And I could never love a girl as dumb as Jodi, so her beauty doesn't stir me.

"Now you girls are the type I need. Decent, smart and beautiful."

Anette, Bette and Joan rolled their eyes to show their weariness at Donna's proposals. Dorret moved her eyes to the teens on the tennis court and forced herself to think of how she was going to seduce Dave on Saturday, or sooner if possible. She should have the house to herself on Saturday. Her parents were supposed to go off to the country-side early that morning and not return before night. She would have all day to seduce Dave; 'juice' him, as Bette would say. She was sure her body would awaken him from Jenny's spell.

Dorret saw herself undressing for Dave, in her bedroom, soca music humming at a low volume from her tape-deck. Dave's eyes glazed over with lust, mouth agape. She'd then help him undress. They would tumble onto her bed and make love for hours. He'd tell her he loved her but had been blind to it all along. She'd smile and stroke his brow and tell him their time had just arrived. He'd be moved near to tears and hold her as if he was afraid she'd disappear. Together they'd drive to his apartment and tell the bitch Jenny to pack and leave.

She'd move in soon after Jenny's departure and begin to redo the apartment. Dave would buy her a big engagement ring. There'd be a grand engagement party with the wedding being announced in the press. She and Dave would live together in bliss. A fairy-tale wedding, pictures splashed in the press. The honeymoon would be pure heaven, and she'd have a honeymoon-baby, a boy, Dave Jnr., who'd look just like his daddy.

She came out of her day-dream with a sigh. She was sure Dave would soon be hers. And then she wouldn't have to worry about the strange effect lesbians like Donna sometimes had on her.

Chapter 23

At four o'clock that Monday evening Jenny and Dave were getting ready for the five o'clock soca show at the Institute. They along with Joe and Joe's girl had slept over at a friend's St. Ann's Bay home after last night's show. They returned to Kingston shortly before ten o'clock this morning.

After a full day of jogging and floor exercises, Dave and Jenny felt refreshed after a midday sleep, a shower and a light dinner. The show they were now getting ready for, was the first of the major carnival's nightly shows in Kingston for the next seven nights of Carnival Week. There were several carnivals vying with each other in Kingston, various live-shows and fetes each night, but this was the major carnival event which had the most impressive line-up of artistes and would be putting on the big Sunday Road March.

At half past four Jenny and Dave left their apartment. Jenny's friends, Anna and Ruth, and Anna's husband rode the elevator down with them. All were headed for the Institute's show.

"Jenny you look good enough to eat," said Anna's ever flirting husband. Jenny was in a filmy jump-suit.

"Jenny isn't the type to be thrilled by your corny flirting," Anna said chastisingly. "Really, Jenny, he didn't show his true colours before marriage. Otherwise I'd have sent him packing."

"Jealousy my dear." He winked at Dave. "Dave why not loan me Jenny? Drown Anna at sea if you want!"

"You might both get a huge surprise," Jenny said, "since Ruth promised to have three muscle men lined up for us tonight."

"Three tall muscular Trinidadians," Ruth nodded.

"Trinidadian's might have originated calypso and carnival as we know it," Dave said, "but they sure can't whine-up like us Jamaican men."

The Jamaica Maritime Institute was located on the Palisados penisula of Port Royal, the same legendary seventeenth century pirates' den of Sir Henry Morgan, once known as the wickedest city on earth. It was a narrow stretch of land, which formed a part of Kingston proper and which enclosed the city's habour. That night's show was to feature the line-up from last night's North coast show along with two other soca artistes. It was scheduled to end at midnight, so many patrons were planning to hit one of the all night soca jams in the city centre, or a reggae dancehall, after midnight.

The show began on time. It was a smash from the word go and many were disappointed when the show ended minutes after midnight: the students who were on week-long holidays were angry.

Mr. Hurt made love to his wife all the while thinking of Jenny. Then, as always, he made a hasty retreat from her bedroom to his own. But tonight sleep refused to come easily as it usually did on such nights.

After a half an hour of tossing in his bed, with images of Jenny in tight, thin gym-wear, Mr. Hurt found himself newly aroused. So, for the first time in many years, he returned to his wife's bedroom for a 'second helping'.

Already clawing at his short pajamas, picturing Jenny's glorious thighs, Mr. Hurt entered his wife's dark room only to see her shadowy form bouncing on the bed, low moans of ecstasy escaping from her throat. It was as if she was being ridden by a ghost. He switched on the overhead lights.

His wife was naked and fucking herself with a vibrator. Indignation filled him.

Mrs. Hurt sprang up with a cry of alarm. Staring stupidly, petrified, as her scowling husband advanced towards her. He tore the vibrator from her trembling hands and saw the name written down both sides.

"Who the hell is Cedric!" He punched her. She fell across the bed. Enraged by the knowledge of being cheated on, Mr Hurt fell on his wife with fists, landing blows to her face and body. She screamed, whimpered, begged for mercy. When he moved away from her, he was exhausted. And with one last glower at her he stormed from the room cursing, and headed downstairs to get drunk.

Mrs. Hurt, tears streaming down her aching and bruised cheeks, staggered over to her full length mirror. Already one eye was badly swollen. Her entire face was red, black and blue and swelling. Her lips were split and growing heavier each second. Her shoulders, breasts and arms, too, were bruised and swelling. She ached terribly.

She staggered over to the door and locked it. Why had she been so careless as to take out her vibrator without first locking the door?

She stumbled to her bathroom, swallowed three aspirins and splashed her face with cold water – painful, but necessary. Returning to her bedroom she turned out the lights and fell into bed.

In the morning, she vowed to herself, she was going to pack and go to Cedric. Her marriage was over. To stay would mean more abuse. It no longer mattered what her priests would do, let them excommunicate her if they wanted.

Mr. Hurt, still furious, and full of plans to give his wife more 'hell', went off to work extra early the Tuesday morning. Divorce wasn't on Mr. Hurt's mind. He was too devout a Catholic to be hasty about ending his marriage. Plus, he mused, there were his sons to think of. Tonight he'd give his wife a proper interrogation, find out who Cedric was and how long he had been her lover. He was, however, certain it wasn't an old affair and was equally sure this was his wife's first affair.

Well, Mr. Hurt mused as he steered his car through the heavy morning traffic, his wife's affair was now over. And he would see to it that she wouldn't be able to take up with another man. He was going to lay down some strict laws and take away her car. He'd confine her to the house under the watchful eye of some middle-aged black maid who hated whites. And Mrs. Hurt was going to spend the rest of her life regretting her folly. He must get a cat-o-nine-tails, as he must never again hit her with his hands, must never again touch her face: A battered face meant gossip. But a 'cat-o-nine-tails' to the body would remain secret.

Hadn't he once heard, Mr. Hurt suddenly recalled as he neared the 'HQ' of his chain of stores, hadn't he once heard that the spine-tail of a sting-ray made a superb whip? He must ask a fisherman...

As soon as her husband had driven away, Mrs. Hurt struggled into a housedress, washed her face and phoned her lover. She told him all that had happened last night and her intent.

"I'll soon be there," her angry lover told her. "Begin packing."

"Cedric, I must warn you that I look terrible," Mrs. Hurt whispered into the phone. That was a fact: her bruises and pain were worse this morning, one eye almost swollen shut, her discoloured lips nearly twice its normal size.

"I would love to get hold of the bastard," Cedric swore into the phone. For a man who had danced to calypso until three this morning he was in good shape just over four hours later. "Just you begin packing my love. I'll help when I arrive."

They hung-up.

Wincing with pain, Mrs. Hurt took out her biggest suitcase and began to pack her most essential items of clothing and make-up. She hadn't packed much by the time she heard Cedric's car screech to a halt at the gate. Gladness gave her new strength and she rushed from her room, and down the stairs. She met the live-in helper heading for the front door. It was obvious that her mistress' battered face shocked her but she asked no questions.

"I am expecting him," Mrs. Hurt whispered through her swollen lips. "Go let him in."

The puzzled maid went to call off the dogs and let in Cedric.

"The prick!" Cedric swore when he entered the living room and saw his lover's battered state.

Mrs. Hurt began to cry. The maid was rooted in the front door watching with great interest.

"Don't cry my love," he soothed, taking Mrs. Hurt in his arms gently. He used his handkerchief to tenderly dry her face. It stung but she didn't wince. She already felt a lot better from being in his arms.

"Mavis," Mrs. Hurt said to the blushing maid. "I am leaving. Take care of the boys. You might not see me for a few days. But I will be near."

The maid nodded. Her heart went out to her mistress. She knew Mr. Hurt had a steady string of young lovers, some school girls. She had seen the notes and pictures they sent him, he was always leering, pinching and groping her. Thank God he hadn't shown any interest in sex with her. Why should he batter his wife because she had a lover? Men were so unjust.

Mrs. Hurt led Cedric upstairs to her bedroom. They packed two suitcases of her clothes and jewelry and a few pairs of shoes.

"Forget the rest," Cedric said. "I'll buy you some new things."

Cedric took a suitcase in each hand. They left the room without a backward glance. She was carrying her make-up case, and the vibrator in a coloured plastic bag. They met her sons on the stairs going down to breakfast — school was on a week's holiday.

"These are my sons," she said. The two lads were gazing at their mother's battered face with incredulity. "Your daddy did this to me last night," she explained, wincing at the pain talking caused. "I am leaving him for good. Remember I love you both. Be obedient to the maid. I'll see you later this week. This is Cedric."

The boys had grasped the whole situation. All those television 'soaps' had given their ten and twelve year-old minds an understanding of domestic disasters. They sympathized with their mother but glowered at Cedric. Cedric gave them a nod and moved on.

The Tuesday morning was overcast when Cedric drove off from Mrs. Hurt's former home. He was sorry she had had to endure a cruel beating but glad that he need not worry anymore about her reluctance to leave her beastly husband.

Still in pain, eyes closed and head against the head-rest, Mrs. Hurt laid her hand on Cedric's thigh. She was in pain but happy about the future.

At the time that Cedric was driving Mrs. Hurt to his house, Jenny and Dave were surfacing from sleep with gentle caresses and vivid memories of last night's sweet, sweet soca. After last night's show at the Institute they had stopped off at the 'socavillage' at one of the smaller carnivals. The 'soca-village' was at Barons plaza on Constant Spring Road and was being used for nightly soca shows and dances during Carnival Week. This morning Dave had no intention of going to work before noon and Jenny was happy to have him lay abed with her.

Down in Kencot, Harry was late for work, but he was full of bounce. Last night he had been at the Institute soca show, and had seen Jenny and her uptown brown boyfriend. He had been tempted to kick the shit out of them both; instead he had kept out of their way, whining instead with the fat brown girl he had escorted. He had a master plan for Jenny. He was sure she and her boyfriend would be in the Road March on Sunday. He was going to drag her out of it, after knocking out her boyfriend with one punch, then flog Jenny straight back to Kencot and show her who was man for a few days before kicking her out. She could then return to her uptown brown man.

On that same Tuesday morning Harry's frisky wife in St. Mary was smacking her thick lips, sitting in her bamboo kitchen. She was full of thoughts of her plans for Harry. God, let her just see him watching the Road March on Sunday and be able to get close enough without him seeing her.

Once he was home again he wouldn't ever be able to leave her side... and oh she was going to ride him, ride him... ride him till he was of no use to another woman.

She squeezed her huge, powerful thighs in gleeful anticipation.

Chapter 24

Paula, the whore who had informed Inspector Hinds of Don J's supposed robbery and kidnapping plan, lived in Kencot. The Inspector never went to her house. She handed over her protection money and information either at the Half-Way-Tree road junction, where she and several other girls usually operated, or at a New Kingston restaurant. She was the head of her little group and was always the one who dealt with the Inspector. She and two of her friends were from Don J's area and often catered to Don J's vast and indiscriminate sexual appetite.

Just after two o'clock on this first Tuesday afternoon of April, Paula phoned Inspector Hinds to tell him she had the name of the person to be kidnapped. As was the norm in such 'hot' cases they spoke in code and arranged to meet at the New Kingston restaurant owned by the Inspector's brother-in-law. Today they met there at 3.30 p.m.

The Inspector, in plain-clothes, arrived first and slipped in through the back to his brother-in-law's cluttered little office. Fifteen minutes later, Paula was shown in.

Paula was a tall buxom thirty year-old whore with slender ankles, dark-brown complexion and short hair dyed a light-brown. Her plain face had the hard but attractive lines of a survivor: she had been working the streets since her mid-teens. Today, in a brown pants-suit, she didn't resemble her glittery night-self. "Is a girl name Bette Fox," Paula told the Inspector as soon as she sat in the chair facing the cluttered desk on which the Inspector was perched. "Hear dem hav' nuff pictures of her, even in de costume she'll be wearin' dis Road March."

124

The Inspector nodded gravely. He knew the girl. She was a damn valuable victim alright. His brother-in-law's stuffy little office suddenly seemed to be closing in on him. Why kidnap the girl out of a crowded Road March instead of at her gate or as she was leaving or entering her workplace? It didn't seem to make sense.

The Inspector knew Paula feared him, where her livelihood was concerned. With Don J, though, she'd fear for her life — and her family's. So it was possible that she was doing Don J's bidding.

Most likely though, the Inspector mused, if Don J was carrying out a hoax he was using Paula as an innocent victim.

In any case, she was all he had. He must trust her. Meanwhile there were dozens of cops and scores of soldiers trying to round up Don J and his gang while simultaneously letting Don J — captured or not — know they had heard about his robbery plans.

Paula was humming a song, while the Inspector thought, her eyes gazing unseeingly out the window at the building next-door. She gave him her full attention as soon as he spoke.

"Look Paula. You did a damn good job. You and your friends can tek' a free run for three months. But," (Paula was glowing with delight), "you could earn my protection permanently free of cost if you can find out whether or not Don J is trying to pull a hoax.

In other words, I suspect he might be lying about intending to kidnap and rob on Sunday in an attempt to keep us occupied while he carries out some other major crime. Understand?"

Paula nodded. "Yea".

"Knowin' Don J," the Inspector resumed, "he won't tell you or anybody else whether or not it's a hoax before Saturday. On Saturday evening or Saturday night he and his gang will feel that it's safe to brag to women about the big day on Sunday. So I want you to try to see Don J Saturday evening, get him to bed an' give him your best. If he has a card up his sleeve he might tell you, especially if he is drunk. Understand?"

"That'll be easy," Paula said with a nod. "Don J is a sex machine. An' always sendin' fo' me to come ball him."

"Good," the Inspector beamed. It occurred to him that her confidence must be due either to her being a part of Don J's plot — whatever it might be — or the prospect of earning the carrot he had just dangled. "I will be at the carnival fete at the Police Officers' Club Sat-

125

urday night. If you learn anything new and get away from Don J before two o'clock that night, you come and find me. I'll be in the bar. If you can't reach there by two o'clock or don't learn anything new, you must phone my house between six and seven Sunday morning. Got that?"

"Sure," she said as she rose with a smile, and with her usual parting shot "Ready to try the best as yet inspector?"

As always the Inspector returned her smile. "I am hooked on my wife girl, hooked totally."

Driving back to his office, Inspector Hinds felt pleased with himself. If the kidnapping rumour was a hoax and Paula willingly a part of the plot, Don J would now think twice when Paula reported to him. If Paula wasn't working with Don J she might learn the truth from Don J Saturday night.

Yes, the Inspector mused, he had played his cards right, and he tended to believe Paula was sincere.

Inspector Hinds' superior officer at the Half-Way-Tree station, Superintendent Mills, was about to leave for home when the Inspector forced his way past the Superintendent's sulky secretary, a brown young lady Corporal who would've been pretty if she'd only be more pleasant.

The 'Supe' glowered at Inspector Hinds' forced entry into his neat and spacious air-conditioned office. "Didn't I say no more visits," "the 'Supe' all but screamed, though he did realise that it was another of Inspector Hinds' 'Dirty-Harry-styled' visits.

The Inspector shut the door on the secretary's whining answer.

"Inspector have you lost your mind?" Thundered the 'Supe,' his fleshy black face murderous, but part of him was praying that the news the Inspector had wasn't too dark.

"Urgent matter Supe," the Inspector said placatingly. "I jus' learn Don J is planning to kidnap Bette Fox out of the Road March."

The Supe slumped backwards into his comfortable swivel chair. "Jesus Christ!" His face was suddenly grey. "And to date not one of his fuck-cloth men have been detained. As for the man himself." He waved his plump arms. "Why the rass did I ever become a cop? I am fifty-seven years old and fuckin' feel like ninety! Now all this." He paused to give vent to a sardonic laugh. "My parents near eighty but they goin' bury me."

Inspector Hinds sat, uninvited, in one of the two chairs facing the 'Supe's' huge uncluttered desk, patiently awaiting the end of the Supe's

126

tirade. He was un-fazed by the outbursts because he knew his boss was a good cop at heart who cared about his staff.

The 'Supe' sighed. "At least we know well before hand." His fingers began to drum on the gleaming surface of his desk. "Thanks to you. We can at least let Don J know we got wind of his nasty plans. That should soil the bastard. Fuckin' skunk. Nothin' worse than a cop turned gangster. Only such a person would think to try something as audacious as to kidnap someone out of a Road March."

The Inspector nodded. He wasn't yet ready to air his suspicion that Don J was setting them up. And he definitely wouldn't tell of the mission he had given Paula.

"Well," the 'Supe' said, rising to his feet, "I shall now go see the Commissioner on my way home. We decided not to broadcast the robbery threat but kidnapping is another matter. The Minister will have to be informed immediately."

Superintendent Jennings at Central is handling the search for Don J and his closest cronies. I shall do my best to see you get the kidnap angle."

"Thanks chief. I would love to handle it." Once again the Inspector gave thanks that the 'Supe' never pressed his detectives for their source of information. He left feeling proud of having done a good day's work.

That night, Dave and Jenny went to a poolside soca fete at the Le Meridien Pegasus hotel. Another enjoyable night. And, like everyone else, they left the fete feeling that this was the hottest carnival ever. Why, there were still five days left and already the very buildings and inhabitants of the city seemed aglow with the sensuous carnival-fever. Driving to work late next morning Dave was sure he could smell carnival in the air. The soca beat seemed to permeate every aspect of life. The radio stations blasted soca twenty-four hours a day, bars pulsed and pedestrians seemed to be stepping in time to the brisk rhythms. Tape-decks in cars and buses blasted soca and the Teens on holidays, held wild, daytime soca parties.

Bette and her 'Troopers,' too, were living in 'carnival heaven'. Except for sexually inactive Dorret, each now had a 'carnival lover'.

On Tuesday morning Jodi's fiancé left the city. She instantly began to work her 'sensual magic' on Carl, enjoying having him constantly drooling over her. Carl was dying for the Road March to arrive so he could blind Jenny.

Natasha and Carmen were hunting Downer pills and Spanish Fly drugs to save the Road March from being wrecked by Carmen's dad when they weren't flirting and seducing men, but wisely practicing safe sex while they were at it.

Pastor Brown was panting for Sunday to arrive, his passion finding an outlet in more intensified sex with his wife.

Mrs. Hurt and her lover were engulfed by happiness, despite her wounds and aches. It was such baccanahalian joy to be able to be with her lover all night and to make love at dawn.

Mr. Hurt was mad over his wife's desertion. Even madder at the knowledge that her lover was younger than her. He had plans to crush that young Cedric. But now, he was horny with carnival-fever, actually having two girls together. He still yearned for Jenny.

Harry was whoring and drinking more than ever. He didn't, though, for a moment think that his fat wife was over in St. Mary full of plans for his recapture. Harry was consumed only with his plan for Jenny.

Chapter 25

It was 11 o'clock when Superintendent Mills arrived at his office Wednesday morning. He was in a crisp khaki uniform and peak-cap. He immediately sent for Inspector Hinds. The Inspector arrived promptly, looking alert in his plaid shirt and pants with white tie.

The Minister and the Commissioner, the 'Supe' told the Inspector, were very grateful for his information and was putting him in charge of security against any possible attack along the Road March route and the kidnap threat. The Minister had notified the press and gotten their promise not to air the matter without the Minister's go-ahead. As a reward for his good work, the Inspector would soon be promoted.

The Inspector was pleased. Very much so. Command of the kidnap case and security along the Road March route were more than he had expected.

He and the Inspector, the Supe added, were to meet the Police High Command at the Commissioner's office that afternoon.

The Inspector hurried home to put on his uniform.

At three that afternoon, Inspector Hinds was in a neat, roomy, air-conditioned office standing at attention before a gleaming conference table. Seated were the Commissioner, two Assistant-Commissioners, three Senior-Superintendents, Superintendent Mills and two stenographers. The Inspector was glad he wasn't asked to sit. He was too damn nervous: Always was with top brass.

The Commissioner commended the Inspector on his fine performance in getting word of Don J's plans for Road March day.

Inspector Hinds managed a not too shaky "Thank you, Sir!"

One of the Assistant-Commissioners then took over! They thought, he said, that letting Don J know his plans were known would most likely put an end to the matter. And efforts would be redoubled to detain Don J and key members of his gang. No need to call off the Road March or frighten the organisers as yet. Bette Fox, the intended kidnap victim, need not be told before Saturday, she and her close relatives and friends would be asked to withdraw from the Road March, although they would be and already were under close surveillance. The Press was cooperating and those in the know had to refrain from spreading the news further afield. Not even colleagues, husbands or wives should be told. In addition there needed to be security measures, in case Don J persisted in trying to kidnap somebody.

Had the Inspector any plans?

"Sirs," Inspector Hinds began, then nodded at the lady Senior Super-intendent," and Madam, first I must say that as one who knew Don J well years ago, I know he is sly, very sly." The Inspectors' nervousness was rapidly evaporating. "I am beginning to suspect that the robbery and kid-nap rumour might be a cover for some other plan he has for Sunday."

All faces became alert. A line of sweat broke out on the Commissioner's black face. He was a man who took all failure by members of his Force personally.

The silence was deadly as minds reeled with speculation at this latest revelation.

Inspector Hinds continued, "My opinion is that we should let Don J think we've taken that bait. Make it known that our teams will be at each road junction along the Road March route and that they would have studied photos of Don J and his closest cronies. However, at the same time we'd have a large security force on alert in case Don J does have a trick up his sleeve.

"Of course, we'd also have plain-clothes men and their informants on look out all over West Kingston from early Sunday morning if we don't detain Don J and his head men by then."

"Inspector you have a sharp brain," the Commissioner nodded. "Your plan is wise. If we let Don J know we suspect he is hoaxing us and it turns out to be true, he could still make his move with extra caution, or put it off for another day. Your way will fill him with confidence enough to make him careless, giving us a strong chance of clipping his wings for good." He sighed. "True, not knowing for sure what he intends means he could still get around us. But it's better to risk it than to have him surprise us on a day when we expect nothing. And we really have no grounds against him strong enough to send him to prison if we detain him before Sunday.

"Your plan at least ensures he won't be able to kidnap anybody or carry out any other attack on members of the Road March.

"Okay Inspector, I will have to see the Minister this evening. Tomorrow afternoon we'll need you to finalise our plans. Be assured you'll be in charge. Meantime, drop all else and see if your sources can learn anything further."

The Commissioner rose.

Inspector Hinds saluted. He left the HQ in high spirits. Promotion was near. Uh-huh, ah-ah. Get ready for the big one Sonia. Uh-huh!

Jenny and Dave went to an 'Old Mas' fete Wednesday night, which was held on the lawns of a small New Kingston hotel. It featured old calypso and dancing and many people were costumed in vintage clothing to match the atmosphere. Jenny and Dave wore black sweat pants and 'slashed' red T-shirts. At midnight they left and went to the Constant Spring Road soca-village fete.

Harry saw Jenny and Dave at the soca-village although Jenny didn't see Harry. He kept to the shadows and out of her way. He wasn't going to confront her until Sunday.

Jodi and Carl, too, were at the soca-village. Jodi was tempted to spring on Jenny and tear her to pieces, but restrained herself, reminding herself that, Carl was going to fix Jenny soon enough. Then she would get back Dave and lead him to the altar.

Inspector Hinds and his family went to the Old Mas fete but left just before midnight. He and his wife then had a riotous time in bed to soca music.

On Thursday, the Inspector returned to the Commissioner's offices at Police HQ and learned that his plan was fully approved. He and Superintendent Mills were given 1000 men - the best chosen from all parts of the country and were to work alongside the Major who would be in charge of the J.D.F's section in operation 'March'.

It wasn't until Thursday that Carmen and Natasha were able to scrounge up a few of the pills commonly called 'Downers' by abusers. They were all set, having found some Spanish Fly Wednesday. The Downers would make Pastor docile while the Spanish Fly would make him horny so they'd get pictures of him erect. Their plans to drug Pastor had to be changed from Friday morning to Saturday as Carmen's mother had phoned Wednesday to say she and Pastor were going off to the country Thursday morning and would be away until Friday evening.

They would be cutting it close, but the girls were confident they would succeed.

Chapter 26

$\mathcal{T}$hursday night was a fine night. It was also a much awaited night as it was the night when the Calypso Tent fete would take place in the car-park of New Kingston's Cinema Two. It was jammed long before the old moon rose upon the city.

Everyone, it seemed, was there.

The gossip writers were there.

Sportsmen, tradesmen, business persons. Union folks, sports-princesses, and that sweet 'black-diamond' Queen of the track. Beauty queens — including she who in a few months would become the first queen of the two major 'beauty-lands' — and models. Doctors and Obeahmen. Reggae stars and super-stars, their managers and producers. Horse trainers and jockeys. The lovely 'Donut' and others of the electronic media. The aerobic queen of television. Nurses and Deacons. Pickpockets and gunmen. Smugglers. Higglers. Tourists.

Yes, they were all there. Colourful and splendid, dressed in everything from the latest fashions, to the older styles, some scantily clad, others modestly covered. Plain faces, faces loaded with colourful make-up. Everyone absorbing calypso/soca.

Big pleasures! Uh-huh! Carnival! Soca, calypso! Huge whining!

This was Mrs. Hurt and Cedric's first venture out of his house since her move there the Tuesday morning. Her swellings and bruises were almost gone. She was satiated and as sore as a virgin bride on her honeymoon.

Dorret's escort was sulking over her refusal to give him sex since their first date. The other girls were letting off on his pals: so why wasn't

Dorret giving him some 'carnival-satisfaction'? She was hot enough on the dance-floor. But what did she expect him to do, go home and masturbate or go buy pussy after each fete?

Frustrated and annoyed by Dorret's attitude, he went to dance with another young lady who made it clear she'd love to go home with him after the fete. He told her she was on. He didn't return to Dorret.

Dorret wasn't put off over losing her escort. His pleas for sex had become tiresome. Like her friends and most other canivalites up to ninety years old, she was as horny as a nympho. But she wanted to save all her energies for Dave, she was eagerly anticipating the seduction she had planned for Saturday and couldn't focus on having sex with any other man right now. Last night she had dreamt he was making love to her, and she had wakened in the throes of an orgasm.

Although being sober and seeing Dave with the black bitch Jenny was disheartening, Dorret was glad she and the girls had sworn not to get drunk after last Sunday night's fiasco, as it was best not to allow Dave to see her drunk again. One consolation was that the music was so sweet that Jenny's presence with Dave couldn't completely dampen her spirits. She, however, had no intention of asking Dave to dance. Saturday would arrive soon enough. Right now, though, she was going to get on that dance floor and take advantage of the many willing dance partners.

Inspector Hinds was nearby in his favourite plaid sports jacket dancing and raving more than ever before, to the delight of his energetic wife. He was exhilarated by his new found esteem with his colleagues and his confidence at outwitting Don J on Sunday.

Dave and Jenny were one happy-soca-calypso-carnival-being. They enjoyed themselves immensely. Gaily dressed in patterned shorts, long white socks, running shoes, black leather sleeveless jackets, and polka-dot head-bands, they drank beer and wine, unable to get drunk because of their sweat-producing dancing.

Each time she saw Jenny and Dave, Jodi was filled with a maddening mix of hatred for Jenny and desire for Dave. It only made her tease Carl harder, on and off the dance-floor. She must make Carl want her so badly that there would be no chance of him getting 'cold-feet' on Sunday, Jodi told herself. She'd deny him sex until Sunday night but maybe tonight she might have pity on him and blow him on the way home.

Carl was aching with lust for Jodi, his erection felt as huge and strong as a crane. He was dying for Sunday's Road March to come, visualizing how he would manoeuver his spear into that bitch's eye. Then Jodi would be his.

Jodi and Carl weren't the only ones plotting misfortune for Jenny. Harry in the shadows, was busily picturing how he would flog her all the way, from Half-Way-Tree Square to Kencot on Sunday.

While Harry was plotting his revenge, his wife in St. Mary was having erotic dreams of him. When she brought him home Sunday she intended to be the dominant one, and she was going to see that she rode him mercilessly...

Mr. Hurt spent Thursday evening at the apartment of one of his single young clerks who incidentally, happened to be his church sister. This wasn't his first twist with her. It was, however, his first time in her bed with her and another girl. The other girl was a model he had brought along. Still, all this wasn't enough to dispel his lustful yearning for Jenny.

Perhaps he could arrange to get Dave out of the way?

The Calypso Tent ended at 1.00 a.m. The hundreds of horny, tipsy couples spilled out onto the streets in a frenzy to get their sweaty bodies home for sex. Wayward teens stopped in parks and dark corners to neck while some went 'all-the-way'. Whores did a brisk business, especially those who had condoms for sale. Teens under strict guidance went home to masturbate. The fete had seemingly stirred up one big orgy.

Dorret intending to get home to satisfy her mounting desire by masturbating, was about to get a lift with Bette and Joan and their escorts, when Donna — the lesbian body-building dentist — offered to drive her home. Knowing that Bette and Joan and their escorts were burning for sex, as much as Anette and her escort, who had already gone off, Dorret accepted Donna's offer.

Donna looked butch in her man-styled pants and sports jacket. "Saw that you were alone," Donna beamed as she drove off, "but you were busy on the dance-floor. I was longing for a dance with you, especially since you were looking ultra-sexy tonight."

Dorret did look ravishing in gold stretch lame tights and white shirt-dress. She blushed, regretting her impulsive acceptance of a lift from Donna so late at night. Donna was a friend but her lesbian passes always made her so damn uneasy.

"What say you to dancing with me?" Donna persisted.

"Don't see how that'll ever be," Dorret managed to say, gazing out the window. She knew it was silly to be unnerved by Donna but something inside, some unknown force, caused it to be so.

Donna was driving slowly through the well lighted major road and her lust was burning hotter by the second. Lately she had found herself thinking that Dorret was to be the final love of her life. She could have carried home any one of several beautiful girls she had seen tonight, but she just couldn't have passed up the chance of being alone with Dorret. She must go slowly though. She didn't expect sex from Dorret tonight. Still...

"There are clubs and parties where women are free to dance together," Donna said. "We can go to such a club right now?"

"Oh no," Dorret responded hastily, still avoiding Donna's eyes. "That's just not my style. Take me straight home, please."

"Anything you say honey pie," Donna coaxed, biting back her disappointment. She had hoped to invite Dorret to her apartment for a drink and talk of lesbian life. " Donna and Dorret mesh so well I won't stop hoping though."

Dorret remained silent. Her heart was pounding. Why was she so scared?

"Dorret dear I swear I won't ever try to force myself on you if you and I were alone. Maybe you could pay me a visit Saturday? Just to talk."

"No. I am sorry, but it wouldn't be wise. I'm not a lesbian." She tried to say firmly, but her voice wavered.

Donna caught the uncertainty in her voice and began to really think she had a chance. Dorret's reluctance she felt was mainly due to fear of what society would say. Someday soon Dorret might need a shoulder to cry on, a sympathetic ear to listen, and she'd be there. She was sure if she could speak to her alone she could break down Dorret's fear of gossips.

For the rest of the journey Donna kept the conversation to the economic situation. Dorret was greatly relieved.

After Saturday, Dorret told herself, I won't need to fear Donna and her muscular body and sexual advances. I will have Dave.

On their way home from the Calypso Tent, Carl tried to talk Jodi into going to a motel. He felt as if he was about to explode with wanting her. He was glad he wasn't driving.

"No love," Jodi coaxed. "Wait until Sunday night. I have plans for an unforgettable night and morning at a motel.

"That is if you prove your love by doing what I asked you to."

"I will, I will! I love you more than life!"

"Then I'll know for sure that you do love me." She took a hand from the steering wheel and placed it on his leg. "You have a wild reputation. And I don't want to be added to your list of broken hearts. Tonight I will give you a treat though." She said suggestively, moving a hand up his thigh.

Carl shivered with anticipation at the promise of a blow job.

He was also pleased that Jodi had heard of his numerous sexual conquests. Over the years he had heard rumours to the effect that Jodi was supposed to be loose with men, but he had never believed them. There was no doubt in his mind that Jodi was a 'proper lady' and he felt that Dave and her fiancé were the only men she had slept with other than himself. Men wouldn't hesitate to try to boost their image by lying that they'd slept with Jodi the great beauty.

"Couldn't we do it in the back seat?" Carl asked after a few moments. "I mean the real thing. It's...."

"Carl! I am not that type of girl!"

She looked and sounded so genuinely hurt. Carl felt a shot of panic which caused him to lose his erection. "Sorry my love! You don't even need to stop to blow me. Forgive me darling?"

"I always keep my promises." She gave him one last frown, then a melting smile.

What a silly boy, she thought. She was headed for a secluded stretch of road beyond their homes, a spot she knew well from her many teenage sexual escapades. It consisted of a vacant lot which grew only crab-grass and broom-shrubs. You could drive in and be hidden from the road. "I'll blow you then go home like the nice girl I am. You are forgiven."

Carl regained his erection.

Jodi loved him, he was sure, but she didn't trust his love, for her. All this would change after Sunday though. He intended to see to that.

Jenny and Dave didn't stop on their two mile drive home from the Calypso Tent fete.

Dave drove quickly, but they still didn't make it to bed before the power of their calypso lust got the better of them. All restraint was lost by the time they got to the living room. Feverishly kissing and groping they fell to the floor, knocking aside the coffee table in the process. They soared to a bacchanalian climax.

It was a simultaneous climax that left them panting and thinking of more sex. They laid there entwined on the living-room rug, silent for half a minute.

"Girl," he said, "that was something special." He sighed.

"Yes, boy, it was one of the 'big' ones." She stroked his back.

"You'd best begin getting ready for a bigger one."

"I'm gonna give you a big welcome."

"Make it huge."

"Going to be huge and sweet, mister."

"My stay is going be long and full of tempo."

"Ah, just the kind I want."

"Despite all you say, I best begin to prepare you." He began to kiss her breasts...

Chapter 27

By Friday, the city of Kingston, was buzzing with rumours of criminal activity intended to coincide with the Road March. The plotters were said to be from West Kingston, although other rumours held that they were gangs from East Kingston and Spanish Town. There was talk of mass robbery and murder, as well as speculations of attacks on Jamaica House and the U.S. Embassy. The press and the Minister of Security were suspiciously silent. Most carnivalites, however, simply dismissed the rumours as idle gossip.

Friday night the Security Minister announced that, in view of the recent rumours surrounding the Road March, there would be a strong military presence at each junction along the route.

He made no mention of the kidnapping or Don J.

At 6 o'clock Saturday morning, Pastor Brown was woken by his wife.

"It's Carmen," Mrs. Brown explained anxiously, hating to disturb him. "She says she must speak to you in person. She sounded so determined I just had to wake you."

With a bone-weary grunt, Pastor eased his tall, muscular, half-naked frame out of bed. Last night his wife had confessed to having lusted after some young man or the other out in the country, and so he had whipped her with the 'holy-belt' - the usual passionate sex had followed. The fleeting thought of last night's activities gave him an erection as he struggled into his too-small bathrobe.

Mrs. Brown saw Pastor's erection and flushed with memories. She had enjoyed the flogging. She had deliberately lied to Pastor about lusting after a young man in the country because it would mean a flogging - and floggings, she knew, were always followed by the wild sex she loved.

"What yu want daughter of satan?" Barked Pastor into the phone in the gloomy living-dining room. The sun wasn't yet fully up on the city, and the windows and curtains were still closed.

"Oh Daddy," came Carmen's half-sobbing reply, "The Lord appeared to me last night. I want to come home to you Daddy, you must come pray with me now. But," Pastor was shocked into speechlessness, happily so, but speechless nonetheless, "but you must come alone, and don't tell Mom as yet; let's surprise her by returning home together later this morning."

Pastor was a man who loved the dramatic. "Sure love, I'll do as you say," he said softly, though his whole being wanted to shout for joy. "Glory to God. I'll be with you within half an hour. We'll pray..."

"And pack my clothes," Carmen intoned solemnly.

"Amen my love. I better hang-up before I begin to shout for joy." His black face was split by an ear-to-ear grin.

"Hurry over."

"Love you."

"Love you sweet dad."

"Never did stop loving you my sweet child."

Pastor hung-up thinking, surely God loved him. What great blessing he had bestowed on him this morning. His prodigal daughter returning home to the Lord!

Pastor had to clench his teeth to keep himself from shouting the good news to his wife. He managed to return to the bedroom with a neutral expression on his face.

"Wife," he boomed, "I have to go out right away. Should be back by nine or so."

"What did Carmen say?"

"When I return you'll hear all about that," he responded evasively. "Be assured it wasn't bad news." He headed off for the bathroom.

Mrs. Brown was sitting on the bed, her aching bum flooding her with more sensual memories of the night. Carmen flew from her thoughts. She wasn't concerned, that Pastor was suddenly in a hurry to go somewhere on some unknown errand. He always had so much to do she preferred not to know the half.

"He swallowed the story hook, line and sinker," Carmen said to Natasha as she put down the phone. They congratulated each other. "He'll be here soon".

"Girl you were impressive," Natasha said. "A oscar winning performance.

"Anyway, the coffee is awaiting him, and so am I."

"Me too."

Carmen was by the front door when Pastor rang the bell twenty minutes later. She took a deep breath to dispel her anxiety and flung the front door open throwing herself into Pastor's welcoming arms.

She was in a modest house-dress. He looked dandy-ish in red pants and a floral short sleeve cotton shirt.

"Oh daddy" She gushed dramatically.

"My daughter!"

He kissed her cheek affectionately, almost squeezing the breath out of her in his enthusiasm.

"Daddy, I am so happy."

"Blessed be The Lord God!"

They went inside holding hands and singing the twenty-third Psalm. In the living room, bright with the strong morning light, they knelt on the rug in front of the sofa. Pastor prayed, several minutes of booming thanks and praise. Half-way through he was shaking with the Spirit, his hands on Carmen's head. Proud of her performance so far, she now began to give vent to an extraordinary show of sobbing and trembling. She played the lost sheep returning to the fold to the hilt!

"...Amen!" Pastor ended his prayer.

"Glory! Oh glory on high!" she leapt to her feet crying and doing a little jig that was a common sight in all Zealous Pentecostal temples.

He leapt to his feet gracefully executing a 'turn-yu-roll', spinning and dipping on one leg.

They sang 'The Prodigal Return', clapping and twirling, dipping and stomping feet, in their fervour.

In her room, Natasha was trying to stifle her laughter in her pillow. She had to get a grip, she thought. Any moment now either Carmen or her Dad will be summoning me.

At the end of the hymn 'The Prodigal Return', Carmen and Pastor fell into a tight embrace. He lifted her off her feet and spun her around as if she were a little girl.

Carmen felt genuine pride in the fact that he was so strong. He sat down on the sofa, settling her on his lap. He was remembering when she was the little girl of his heart; now he was overjoyed at the prospect of having her close to him once more. "When you was a little lass a use to love havin' you like this," he declared, "the boys at my feet, while I read bible stories."

She kissed his sweating black brow. "Well, you are so big and strong I will never be too big for your lap."

"And dad," she said, resting her head against his massive chest, "I don't think I shall ever marry. I want to dedicate myself to the church."

"Daughter, The Lord will guide your steps." He was partly pleased with the thought of her always being by his side — but at the same time he knew it was almost always best for the righteous to marry.

"You'll see," she said, nuzzling his shoulder, enjoying her role immensely. "From now on your home is mine. Wherever you go I go, your every word my command, and in your old-age I'll be your maid."

A wave of tender emotions overcame Pastor. "Oh my beloved, most blessed daughter." He began to sob his gladness, rocking back and forth. His daughter had returned.

"Now let us drink some coffee," Carmen said, "then we'll pack some of my clothes and go rejoice with Mom."

"She's going to be as overjoyed as I am," Pastor said, drying his tears. "Go get us that coffee." Coffee was one of his few weaknesses; coffee four or five times a day wasn't unusual with him. "Where is your room-mate."

"In her room. Natasha come here! I hope she'll see the light of The Lord soon." She sighed piously.

"We'll pray for her."

Natasha entered the room looking shy and bewildered.

"Come say hello to Dad while I fetch some coffee," Carmen said to her be-robed flat-mate. "Want some?"

"No thanks," Natasha responded.

Carmen went off to the small kitchen. There were two pots of coffee there waiting. The pot with the yellow handle was safe. The pot with the red handle held danger.

Natasha sat in the wing-chair to Pastor's left. Pastor started expounding the tenets and aim of his church as she feigned enthralled interest.

Carmen was back in a jiffy with a cup and a large mug: Both held coffee. She gave her dad the mug and sat down sipping hers.

"Good of you to give me a mug. I hate those little cups!" Pastor took a good mouthful of his coffee. "Just the way I like it. Hot and strong, with lots of milk. You remember your old Dad well."

"Because I love him," Carmen said, beaming, satisfied that he didn't taste the drugs in the spiked coffee.

" Dad," Carmen said," my leaving will put Natasha in a bind. So..."

"Carmen please," Natasha protested on cue. "Something will work out."

"Of course," Pastor said, "Carmen must continue to pay half the rent until you find a new room-mate or a smaller place."

"She will not right now be able to find a new room-mate," Carmen said, "and living alone would drive her crazy." Dad must be kept talking and thinking, so he wouldn't be aware of the drug too quickly.

"Oh Carmen, really!" Natasha said.

"Natasha I know you well," Carmen said. "Daddy, she thinks that you and Mom wouldn't be pleased if she were to come live with us and continue going to her Baptist church and parties."

"Carmen!" Natasha rolled her eyes in embarrassment.

"Dear Natasha," Pastor said paternally, "I can understand why you might think that most older Christians are so narrow minded. But I assure you that my wife and I aren't like that." (Yeah, right??!! Carmen thought sarcastically). "One third of the people we help," Pastor continued, "are not of our church." At least this was a fact "Come live with us, you are Carmen's sister, so to speak . I won't force my religion on you and you can continue to live your personal life as before."

"I'll think about it," Natasha said.

"Fair enough," Pastor said after another huge swallow of his coffee. It would be wonderful, he thought, to win Carmen's best friend over to his

143

flock. If Natasha came to live with them it would be an easy task now that Carmen was re-born.

Carmen was watching her Dad closely, looking for signs that the drugs were taking effect.

Pastor felt even more euphoric with each swallow of coffee, but he attributed that to the joy of the morning. Ah, life was wonderful. He felt as free and as light as a bird. His thoughts moved to last night's pleasures with his wife; he was unable to stop the vivid memories from flooding his mind.

He drained the last of his marvellous coffee.

Carmen and Natasha exchanged knowing glances as they observed the change which had come upon Pastor. His eyes were glossy and his smile growing and his shoulders slumped.

The Downer was working.

Carmen took the empty mug from Pastor's hands. He gave her a sensual grin, thinking she was his wife, reliving the vigorous flogging he had given her last night. The memory of her broad, fleshy backside had him smacking his lips.

Carmen nodded to Natasha.

Natasha went to take the key from the locked front door, and returned to stand behind Pastor.

"Daddy," Carmen said tentatively. He looked at her with a wide grin, thinking how much she resembled her mother. He mumbled incomprehensibly and sank lower in the sofa. He felt so serene and mellow.

"Better than we expected. He won't be any trouble." said Carmen over his head to Natasha.

Natasha hurried to her room.

A minute later Carmen led the docile Pastor to Natasha's crowded blue and white bedroom. Pastor grinned at Natasha; he wasn't sure who she was but thought she was pretty. The girls got him into bed and took off his clothes. Carmen felt a bit embarrassed — after all, this was her father. Natasha stripped and got in beside Pastor. He was already stiffly aroused — Spanish Fly and visions of his wife as a young woman at work.

Carmen took up the instamatic camera. She took some suggestive pictures of Natasha and Pastor in various poses on the bed. There was no denying who the man was, and he and the young lady looked to be burning with passion.

144

Carmen giggled, embarrassed, while Natasha 'wanked' Pastor to a climax — "We can't leave him like this," she had explained.

Then, much to the girls' relief, Pastor instantly fell asleep. They tied his wrists to the sturdy bedhead, put on his underpants and covered him with a thin blanket.

Pastor was a strong man. He woke some fifteen minutes before noon, groggy but sober. Where was he? And why were his hands tied? He heard cars and children outside.

After a minute of dazed thought, Pastor recalled Carmen's phone-call, coming to see her, praying and singing with her...

"Hi dad," Carmen said, entering the room ahead of Natasha. "Sorry about this but I had to do something about your plans for tomorrow."

It all suddenly hit Pastor. She had tricked him, and given him drugged coffee. "You witch!" He bellowed. "Are you going to kill me?"

"I am not that evil," Carmen laughed.

Pastor tried to break free of the ropes binding his wrists to the sturdy bed headboard. He couldn't free himself.

"We took some pictures of you in bed with a girl," Carmen said. "Here is one. The rest are with a friend in the building."

After one glance Pastor shut his eyes against the horror of the photo of his leering face hovering above a young lady's hairy crotch. Natasha's, he was sure.

"Call off your protest march," Carmen said, "and I'll destroy the pictures. Go ahead with it and the pictures go public."

"Of course, you could defy me by telling the truth of the matter — how I tricked and drugged you. But to do so would be to kill Mom."

All the fight went out of Pastor. He could bear public humiliation, but he loved his wife far too much to ask her to live with such a scandal involving their own daughter. He wouldn't even share the secret with his wife. Just hearing about it would wound her dangerously. And Christ said man must love his wife as He loved the church.

Pastor looked up at his unsmiling daughter. "You win. May God have mercy on your soul. An' I will continue prayin' for your return to my flock. 'Cause no matter what, you are my flesh an' blood an' a will always love you as such."

Silence hung in the gloomily lit room, the shriek of playing children outside and music from the apartment above seemed a part of the hum of silence.

Pastor began to weep, sobbing out a doleful rendition of "When I Survey The Wondrous Cross On Which The Prince Of Glory Died."

Carmen felt a stab of shame and guilt. She had to fight back tears. It occurred to her that her dad was, certainly at this point in time, a better person than she and most persons would ever be. But she had to, she told herself, she had to save the Road March.

Natasha fled from the room in tears, ashamed of herself and knowing how deeply Carmen was chastened by her Dad's show of integrity.

Carmen released her father and left him to dress.

A few minutes later at the door, he turned sad, disappointed eyes on her. Carmen wanted to sink to her knees and beg his forgiveness. But she didn't. Then he was gone, and she was reaching out as if after a ghost. She dissolved into tears of deep regret and remorse. Natasha was also weeping. Carmen was still convinced she had done right to save tomorrow's Road March but not sure it was worth the loss she felt.

Chapter 28

While Pastor was leaving his daughter's apartment, hundreds were gathering on the spacious grounds of the Police Officers Club on Hope Road for the early afternoon start of the Kiddies Carnival Road March. Bands of costumed children danced through the streets to calypso music on their march to the New Kingston cinema where there would be a fete for the young and young-at-heart.

A few minutes after noon, Dorret was about to make her third call of the day to Dave. The first and second, at 9.30 and 11, had got no answer and no busy signal, and she had rightly assumed Dave and Jenny were still abed after all night party'ng.

Dorret was alone at home. Her parents had gone off to the country that morning. She had stayed home last night, pleading a headache. She had wanted a full night's rest to be at her best today.

After her parents' departure just before 7.30 a.m. Dorret had done half an hour of exercise. Next she prepared a hearty breakfast and forced herself to eat it - now that the day of seduction was here she was nervous: what if Dave was sick after last night's partying?

After breakfast she had had a long perfumed bath, then lotioned her body and painted her nails a brilliant red. Next was the 9.30 phone call to Dave's apartment.

Getting no answer she hung-up after the sixth ring, sure Dave and Jenny were still asleep. She then did her face, adding long lustrous false lashes and a touch of shimmery eye makeup to make her eyes glitter like diamonds. Then she put on her skimpiest shorts — a white one which set off her shapely, golden-brown legs quite well — and a barely-there, red halter-top. She finished off the ensemble with a delicate pair of strappy sandals. All at completed to her satisfaction, she next touched up her newly bobbed and waved 'bottle' chestnut-brown hair.

She was pleased with what she saw in her full length mirror: a trim, shapely princess no man could resist.

Dorret made her second call at eleven. Again she got no answer. But she still didn't panic. She'd wait an hour before trying again.

Now, at a few minutes after twelve, Dorret's third call met with success as Jenny answered the phone. This pleased Dorret.

"Jenny, it's Dorret." Her tone was distressed. "I need Dave's help to-day, now. A problem my parents and friends wouldn't understand. Please, is he there?"

"Yes," Jenny responded sympathetically, in spite of the fact that the caller was Dorret, who had never been particularly friendly towards her.

"I need for him to come see me here." She sounded on the verge of tears.

"Want to talk to him?"

"Yes, please."

Dave, fresh out of the shower, picked up the phone and listened. "I'll be there in half hour or so," he promised soothingly. He thought it best not to ask for details over the phone. The poor girl sounded so shaken, it would be better to wait until he was with her.

"I knew you wouldn't fail me," Dorret sighed and sniffled. She was glad he wasn't asking what the problem was.

"That's what friends are for."

They both hung-up.

Dave ate breakfast quickly, wondering what had upset Dorret so much. Thoughts of an unwanted pregnancy and AIDS sprang to his mind as he drove through the busy scorching streets to Dorret's home in Meadowbrook.

Dorret was on the veranda of her bungalow home when Dave came to a screeching halt at the gate and jumped out of his car. He was dressed casually but in Dorret's eyes looked like a knight in shining armour rushing to a maiden's rescue.

Dorret ordered the dogs to the backyard as Dave briskly, strode up the short drive-way. He was pleased to see that she looked in good health. She was pleased to see that he seemed in as good a shape as he had sounded over the phone, not the least hung-over from partying and too little sleep.

"Thanks for coming so quickly," Dorret said, sounding and looking as nervous as she suddenly felt. "Let's go inside." She took his hand and led him inside. She closed the front door and smiled nervously at his puzzled brown face. "Dave... I am alone today, will be all day... and I just had to tell you of the love I have been hiding for years."

An incredulous look shadowed Dave's face. He looked intently at her to see if she was serious.

"First you chose Bette," Dorret was blurting out with downcast eyes, "then it was Anette and Joan. Next was Jodi. I tried to show how much I cared for you, especially after Jodi, but you never seemed to understand. Until now I was too shy to say it. Well" — she looked up into his eyes, her breathing heavy. She had to lean against the closed front door for support — "I still love you and can't bear to go on without you any longer."

Silence. Heavy. Dorret felt glued to the door.

Dave stood there in the airy living room staring speechlessly at Dorret. He was dumbfounded. The six feet of glistening grey-green tiles between them seemed like six miles of ocean. Once he had thought he loved Bette. Then Anette and Joan had been amusing flings. Jodi's beauty and sexual skills had mesmerised him. But Dorret?

Dorret?

Dave had always seen Dorret as the perfect 'virginal-tease' and 'spiritual-sister' who would create waves on the dance-floor but deny a man sex until there was either an engagement or months of frustrating petting in cars. And there were always more willing girls. Dave was your typical late twentieth Century man who couldn't love a girl he hadn't known as a lover in bed. Neither did Dave ever have patience for months of petting without sex. So he had kept Dorret at arms length — dancing, flirting and innocent kisses. He wouldn't even be surprised to learn that now in her late twenties she was still a virgin.

Now here she was saying she had been in love with him for years. Unbelievable.

It occurred to Dave that he might have fallen for Dorret if she had been less a prig and tease — she was worse than her friends in both areas, always had been. She was beautiful and bright. But far too priggish. Prigs bored and angered him.

"Dave," Dorret implored, lips trembling. Why wasn't he smiling and hugging her?

"Dave... do you understand?" She advanced on him, her arms spread.

To Dorret's horror Dave backed up sharply and said " Dorret it's far too late. You are not my type. And I love Jenny. I intend to ask her to marry me, soon."

Dorret jerked to a frozen halt. Her face lost all colour under the light coat of make-up. Disbelief and humiliation. Then an image of Jenny's black face came to her. He was talking of marrying the black bitch, after listening to her declaration of love. He was a prick, a bloody inhuman beast! How could she have thought she loved him, a foolish prick?

Indignation surged through her, flooding her neck and cheeks with new colour. She turned and opened the front-door. "Get out you pig! Go to your black bitch!"

Dave hurried past her. He was glad of her show of anger. For a moment he had been scared she'd resort to threats of suicide. That would have placed him between defeat and madness.

As most men would, Dave felt that spurning a woman's love was to belittle himself, diminish his manhood.

Though still indignant, Dorret began to weep silently as she watched Dave hurrying to his car without a backward glance.

Just as Dave drove off, Donna's car pulled up. Dorret felt torn in two — happy to see Donna, and afraid.

At the same time that Dave was with Dorret, Jenny was talking to a distressed Pastor Brown.

Having left the apartment to go for a walk, Jenny almost bumped into the huge black man who stepped around from the side-walk to her left. Like her, he was walking slowly with his head down lost in thought. For a moment she thought he was Harry. A thought which scared her so much she gasped and stepped backwards. She relaxed when she saw that it was only a doleful looking stranger.

Since leaving his daughter's apartment, Pastor had been driving around aimlessly. Gradually his initial decision to forgive Carmen and Natasha without seeking revenge had given way to anger and desire for vengeance against them. But, he had to do it in such a way that his wife wouldn't learn about or even suspect what Carmen and Natasha had done to him.

Five minutes ago, Pastor had parked his car in Jenny's neighbourhood and gotten out to walk around a bit. Now he apologized in somber tones. "Sorry," he said. "Just parked my car so I could wander around."

150

Jenny sensed he had a lot on his mind. She saw too from his appearance, that he wasn't someone she'd need fear, least of all here on a Saturday afternoon in this upper-middle class neighbourhood with people in sight on verandahs.

"Not your fault entirely," Jenny said kindly.

Pastor felt an instinctive liking for this girl in front of him. He saw that she didn't know who he was. It didn't matter to him who she was; Her manner suggested she was a nice person. In fact, she resembled a favourite aunt of his, who'd died young. All these factors and the burning need to confide in someone made Pastor blurt out, "My own daughter, about your age, hurt my soul real bad this mornin'; so bad that as much as I love her I thinkin' of breakin' her neck, or doin' somethin' that'll ruin her career. But whatever I do, my wife must not know what took place this mornin'."

The depth of his despair touched Jenny. They were still standing face to face. "Let's walk," she said hoping it would clear his head.

He gladly fell into step with Jenny.

"The important thing is that you love your daughter," Jenny said. "And you surely know that we younger ones tend to be rash even at the best of times. So you must forgive your daughter. If you must punish her it should be in some way which will not hurt her physically or socially or ruin her career. You know that if you do that you'd only be hurting yourself because you love her so much. Plus you'd be in danger of losing her forever. Then you'd never be able to forgive yourself.

Forgive her, and time will heal your present wound. Then, most likely, you'll find her loving you more than ever."

Pastor didn't respond. He and Jenny walked on in silence.

Jenny was thinking: I envy this man's daughter. He obviously loves her a lot. I wish mine loved me even one-third as much.

Realizing the wisdom of Jenny's advice, Pastor said, "You're right,"

Stopping to face Jenny, he put out his hand. "God bless you." They shook hands. Jenny felt happy for him and his daughter, "That's my car," he said, pointing to his car about seventy metres ahead.

"I'll turn back here, then," Jenny said. He nodded then smiled goodbye. They didn't know each other's names, but they were friends.

It was the spirit of carnival that had made it possible for her to say the right things so easily, Jenny thought.

Chapter 29

Donna was frowning upon seeing Dave driving from Dorret's gate. Didn't he have a girl?

And surely Dorret wouldn't...

Then Donna looked and saw Dorret's shadowy outline, slumping dejectedly in the door-way.

Donna's pulse quickened with excitement. She thanked the gods for the impulse which had led her here this Saturday morning. She rushed out of her car, through the gate, up the short drive-way to her heart-throb. Her heart leapt for joy when she was close enough to see that Dorret was weeping silently. It took a lot of effort to keep herself from smiling. It seemed Dorret was home alone, what a bonus!

"Hello honey," Donna said.

"Hi Donna," Dorret sobbed, hating herself for not being able to stop crying. She meekly allowed Donna to take her hand and lead her inside, to the living area sofa.

"Tell the one who loves you all about it," Donna coaxed, sitting close beside Dorret hugging her. Donna felt she could come on strong, sure that Dorret was as ripe for a lesbian seduction as any girl could be. "Did the prick hurt you?" In fact she had always liked Dave and now loved him even more for making Dorret so vulnerable.

"I hate him," Dorret sobbed. She allowed Donna to draw her closer and caress her back.

"Men are like that." She said in a soothing tone. She must get Dorret to her place before somebody else came along. Strike while the iron is hot! Her clit was stiff, her nipples tingling and hard.

Dorret began to feel calmer and more secure in Donna's strong embrace.

Donna dried Dorret's tears and said. "Let us go for a drive. That'll help."

"Yes," Dorret said. She was thankful that Donna wasn't pressing her for details as to how Dave had distressed her.

They locked up the house and left in Donna's car. Donna wisely took the shortest route to her Constant Spring Road apartment, driving fast and chatting about her plans to expand her Dental services.

Dorret knew what was coming but was unable to resist going where Donna led. She suddenly didn't care what others might think and say. For the first time she was seeing Donna as her guide, teacher and protector.

Dorret was smiling as she and Donna left Donna's apartment at three o'clock that afternoon. Dave and all else were of the unimportant past. Donna was so strong and tender, so skilled at piloting their bodies to unbelievable heights of pleasure. They would be happy. She cared not what her friends and gossips would say.

Donna was walking on air. She had found the love of her dreams. They were now going to fetch some of Dorret's clothing. Tomorrow or next weekend they'd get the rest.

It was Dorret who had suggested moving in with Donna immediately.

By four-thirty Dorret and Donna had packed half of Dorret's clothes into their cars, not bothering to use suitcases. Now they were in the kitchen cooking and awaiting the return of Dorret's parents. Dorret didn't care what her parents would think. Stew all, except what her lady Donna wished!

At five o'clock Bette and her two 'Troopers' — Joan and Anette — came by in Joan's car to find out why they hadn't been able to get hold of Dorret by phone all afternoon. All three were stunned to see Donna's car on Dorret's drive-way, knowing Dorret's parents weren't home. They were even more surprised when they saw piles of Dorret's clothes, shoes and bags strewn on the back seat of Donna's and Dorret's cars. Bette and her two 'Troopers' realised what was afoot. Still, they were bowled over speechless when they were met at the front-door by a glowing Dorret in the possessive embrace of Donna.

For the first time in memory Bette felt herself not in control.

"Hi girls," Dorret beamed with a new lilt to her tone. "I am sure you girls have already guessed. I am going to live with Donna." She felt proud of her avowal, after all she was in love.

"Soon there'll be wedding bells," Donna declared and hugged Dorret closer. She was amazed by the swift about turn in Dorret — already Dorret was ready to defy all who disapproved of lesbians.

"You bet," Dorret said, smiling at her lover.

Bette, Anette and Joan knew not what to say: in fact they felt as if they had been caught doing some grave wrong. Dorret not only sounded different, she looked different! What had come over her? Was Donna some form of witch or what?

"Bette," said Dorret, sounding so unlike her old frail self, "does my new self mean I shall be fired?"

Bette instantly regained her wits. "Of course not. Haven't I always treated Donna as a friend? Why should I allow you to lose your job? I am hurt that you thought it necessary to ask such a question."

"I suppose our friendship will change but I'll make sure Dad doesn't fire you. And soon I'll be one of the top bosses. You are still my friend."

"I won't try to take Dorret's friendship away from you girls," Donna assured sincerely. "We can all be friends," her eyes twinkled," especially now that I don't need to make passes at you girls!"

Anette and Joan nodded. Bette forced a smile.

All five ladies went inside for a few awkward minutes of chat about carnival. Then Bette, Anette and Joan fled.

When Dorret's parents arrived home at dusk they were met by the determined couple. Dorret's father was amused. Her mother, though, was instantly hysterical, worried about what acquaintances would say behind her back. Dorret ignored her mother's tears and pleas and after a few more minutes, Dorret and Donna got into their cars and drove off into the night.

Chapter 30

At dusk that Saturday evening, Mr. Hurt was living one of his favourite fantasies: being in bed with two lovely young ladies. This evening, one was brown, the other black. Earlier they had danced for him in the costumes they'd be wearing in next day's Road March.

Now panting his way to his usual quick climax, having the brown girl doggy fashion and the black one licking his balls, Mr Hurt felt a sudden intense pain in his chest. His mouth opened, his dick lurched, and he was dead before he could scream.

It was the girls who eventually screamed.

Across the city Mrs. Hurt and her lover were playing bondage unaware that now she was a very rich widow.

Dusk saw Jenny and Dave getting ready for the 'Clash Of The Giants, Jamaica vs Trinidad', set to begin at 7.30p.m. at the Police Officers club not far from their apartment.

Upon his hasty return, Dave with disbelief and not a little amusement, told Jenny what had transpired at Dorret's. Jenny's reaction had been a mixture of rage and pity, but that soon evaporated, moved by Dave's fidelity to her. He loved her so much, Jenny's heart soared, that he had passed up a chance to take advantage of a beautiful girl.

The loving Jenny gave him in the late afternoon, made Dave feel like a million dollars.

Bette got an unexpected visit from two of Inspector Hinds' Detective Sergeants not long after her shower at dusk. The uniformed detectives told her of their suspicion that a gang 'might' try to kidnap her tomorrow during the Road March. Though security would be tight they informed her, they must insist that she and her relatives withdraw from the Road March.

Bette's parents were too alarmed to ask more probing questions. But Bette, calm as ever, brain ticking away asked, "Why are the supposed kidnappers planning to take me out of the Road March instead of any of a dozen easier ways?"

The cops having been coached on how to answer that question replied that it was likely just idle rumour but it was best to take it seriously. Many gangsters are deranged and loved the dramatic.

Bette assured the cops she had no relatives who would be in the Road March and she promised to withdraw herself and her close friends.

"The matter must be kept quiet," one officer cautioned her, "to prevent panic, please make sure you tell only your three close friends and make sure they in turn don't tell even their parents or boyfriends."

Bette and her parents agreed to do as the cops said, and listened intently to their plans for the Road March route.

Bette was more amused than frightened and left home early to alert her friends to the danger and the need for discretion. They all vowed not to tell anyone else until after the Road March and said a reluctant goodbye to taking part in tomorrow's Road March.

The girls went to the night's big soca blowout in Bette's car, with Dorret and Donna following closely in Donna's car. They were amongst the first wave of starry eyed patrons to enter the spacious grounds of the Police Officers Club, quite a while before the live show began. There was a disco blasting old calypso hits during the period leading up to the live show.

Inspector Hinds, in striped shirt and plaid pants, introduced himself to Bette. He took her aside and went over what he knew his two sergeants had told her. Bette assured him she and her friends would quietly withdraw from the Road March and wouldn't even so much as tell the guys they were now dating.

The Inspector expressed his faith in her and her friends and again reassured her that they were doing everything in their power to ensure her safety.

With Carnival Week so near its climax, Kingston city was throbbing with musical sensuality, a horny city where every second that Saturday night saw at least one man or woman achieving an orgasm —

clothed, naked, on dance-floors, in bars, in bed, in cars, on grass, carpets and bare floors, sitting, standing, even walking — a great big continuous bacchanalian orgasm, a carnival of sheer raw pleasure. Savage, barbarous, yet so civilized and tender. So intense, that even the dogs, cats and ghosts caught the pulsing sexual fever. When the half-moon rose on Kingston late that Saturday night, it rose to the thunderously passionate mix of soca-calypso-reggae music and sexual climactic cries, gasps, groans, grunts, whispers, it gave the urban carnality a golden hue, it beheld a thousand stiff clits and nipples and caressed a thousand erections and runting buttocks.

Whores felt truly ecstatic that night, some achieving orgasms for the first time in years. Sincerely enjoying their job as they had never thought possible.

But there was one lone whore whose whoring stood a chance to save Kingston from a blood-bath next day; a blood-bath which would kill Carnival Week's Sunday climax with far more horror and surety than Pastor Brown had intended.

The name of this whore was Paula.

Chapter 31

It was 10.43 p.m. when Paula was finally able to get away from Don J and his blonde US girl. They had been at the uptown apartment since late afternoon, mostly in bed. The apartment belonged to Don J's girl, who was a young bisexual coke-head heiress from New Jersey. Don J had been hiding there for the past two weeks, while most of his men were in hiding in various sections of the city and in neighbouring rural districts. This was why the hundreds of cops looking for them in West Kingston had found only a few.

Meeting with Don J that afternoon had been mainly the man's doing. Paula had gone to his west Kingston HQ Friday evening only to learn that he wasn't around. Then this morning he had phoned her to say one of his men would pick her up in the midday to early afternoon period. "Been tellin' me US girl how hot yu are," Don J had explained, "an' she jus dyin' to meet you."

So Paula had been ferried to the posh uptown apartment in the afternoon by one of Don J's 'harmless-boys' whose job was not to take part in the violent criminal activities, but to function as a 'mover'.

Don J's US girl turned out to be tall and trim with a grating voice. Paula disliked her at first sight. All three of them went straight to bed, Paula giving them her best acts.

Don J was an occasional coke user, a man of strong will who could not be called a drug-head. He was not hooked but his girl was. It wasn't until night had fallen that Don J took the first of several snorts of coke with his insatiable girlfriend. Don J's girl passed out just after

9.30. Don J took this opportunity to boast of his 'true' plans for tomorrow.

Paula, who never touched coke or other hard drugs, and had drank very little of the wine, took in with rapt attention all of his devious plans for tomorrow.

The Inspector had guessed correctly. Don J had a secret plan; The kidnap robbery rumour was just a hoax.

Paula had to get to the Inspector. Leaving wouldn't be a problem. Two of Don J's boys were coming for him at 11:00 that night and he'd never suspect her of squealing to the police. He trusted her more than anyone else in the world. Besides, he was so high he wouldn't remember that he had let the cat out of the bag..

Paula left by taxi at 10.43. She told the taxi-driver to hurry her to the show at the Police Officers Club on Hope Road.

"Yu kinda late," the driver said and set off at a fast pace.

Paula leaned back in the back seat and thought about what she had to tell the Inspector. For the past three weeks a white foreigner had been in the Central Lock-up in downtown Kingston, on a gun and drug charge. He had been found travelling with an automatic pistol and several grams of coke in a rented car uptown. He was supposed to be a German tourist. He did speak German, but his German passport and drivers licence had proved to be false. The cops were trying to get a fix on him.

And some unknown source was paying Don J a fortune to get 'The German' out of jail and onto a private jet. Don J had already received half the huge fortune via Switzerland; the rest to be paid when he handed over the fugitive.

Don J's surmise was that the fugitive, 'The German', was a top Mafia Boss who was wanted on all continents and had had a recent 'face-job', with matching doctored passports and other papers. But in time the F.B.I., Scotland Yard and Interpol would solve the riddle. The fugitive's cronies had no contact in Jamaica they trusted to get the cops at Central to 'spring' the fugitive and see to his safe removal out of the island. But they knew about Don J and trusted him to do the job for the right price. Don J's price was huge. Three million US dollars.

The Americans who had approached Don J had helped him to formulate the plan for Road March day.

The plan was this — spread a rumour of robbery or kidnapping to

159

coincide with the Road March to draw the cops' attention to the Road March. What was to coincide with the Road March was an attack by thirty heavily armed men on the General Penitentiary (GP), which would draw cops away from the nearby Central station and other stations in the downtown area. Then minutes after the attack on GP began, a grenade, smoke canister, M16 and sub-machine gun attack would hit Central from two sides, and Don J would lead ten men into the jail area to snatch the prized fugitive while twenty men covered them with heavy fire. Five of the ten men Don J would lead to the jail area were ex-US Marines. The men picked to attack the GP knew nothing of the attack on Central, and most of those to attack Central thought Don J was planning a robbery spree.

As Paula now sped towards the Police Officers Club thinking of these things, the five ex-Marines were in a Kingston 5 bungalow, checking their bullet-proof vests, grenades, smoke canisters and submachine guns.

The rest of Don J's men were already gathering in Two East Kingston ghettos from whence they would spring their attack tomorrow.

Chapter 32

Jenny and Paula had first known each other from when they were living in West Kingston and continued to remain friends after their individual moves to Kencot. Jenny had never cared for prostitutes, but she saw Paula as being somehow different from others. There was a certain dignity about Paula, and she was polite and kind. Plus, Jenny and Paula's youngest sister had been classmates in Primary school. So now seeing Paula passing by her and Dave at the Police Officers' Club, Jenny called to her. Jenny and Dave were standing together, his arm casually about her shoulder. There was a band change on, and a disco was playing old and new calypso hits.

"Hi Paula," Jenny said.

"Jenny," Paula responded. "How are you." This must be the uptown man Jenny left Harry for, Paula thought. Good for Jenny. She was always bright.

"This is my boyfriend Dave," Jenny was saying. Paula and Dave nodded at each other. " Know who I just saw?" Jenny asked . "Just saw those sisters of Don J."

Paula gasped, despite herself. She felt a chill of dread run through her. She had to make sure Don J's sisters didn't see her talking to the Inspector tonight. Perhaps Jenny and her boyfriend could help?

Even in the dim light, Jenny saw Paula's fear.

"What, are you at odds with the bitches?" Jenny asked above the blast of calypso emanating from the disco's large boxes. On stage the band change was nearing completion.

Paula leaned closer to Jenny's ear. "No. But a must se' a Inspector about some nasty plans Don J has for tomorrow, so it best not to let him sisters se' me talkin' to the Inspector tonight."

"A problem?" Dave asked.

Paula decided she could trust Dave. "Can we go to your car where yu will hear me better?" she asked.

"Let's go Dave," Jenny implored. "It's urgent."

They went off to the parking area. There were couples entwined in some cars but none near Dave's. They sat on Dave's car trunk, Jenny and Dave on either side of Paula. Here the music was far off enough to make conversation comfortable. Paula gave a brief but vivid account of Don J's plan and Inspector Hinds' position.

Dave and Jenny were shocked by the implications of it all. Moments passed before Dave was able to say " I know Inspector Hinds. He once handled a case involving the murder of a close friend of my Dad's."

"It really wouldn't be wise for Don J's sisters to see Paula talking to the Inspector tonight," Jenny said. "Tomorrow when the cops nab Don J they'd become suspicious."

"What we'll do is this," Dave said. "I'll go tell the Inspector he can see Paula at our place. It's near and we will go first, then he can come later."

"Dat will be perfect!" Paula said.

The band change was over and Byron Lee and the Dragonaires band was-now belting out a popular hit. The thick crowd of patrons returned to life, singing and shouting along. Dave and Jenny, though, had lost the carnival spirit in face of the knowledge that tomorrow could bring a lot of deaths. They returned to the show area. Jenny and Paula were waiting near the gate as Dave went off to the bar to discreetly explain Paula's dilemma to Inspector Hinds. The Inspector promptly agreed to be at Dave's apartment in forty minutes.

Exactly forty minutes later, Inspector Hinds arrived at Dave's apartment. He was all nerves fearing the worst. The Inspector actually trembled when he heard Paula's news. He immediately placed a call to Superintendent Mills' home, hauling the 'Supe' out of sleep; and the 'Supe' in turn hauled the Commissioner out of a restless sleep. Inspector Hinds rushed back to the Police Officers' Club to place his wife and two teenaged daughters in the hands of a Detective Sergeant before driving to Supt Mills' home.

Hinds, Supt Mills, the Commissioner of Police and two of his assistants, the Minister of National Security and five top officers of the JDF.

Meanwhile, Jenny and Dave had lost their appetite for further revelling that night. They didn't return to the show, instead they convinced Paula to spend the night on their sofa. Paula had wanted to go home, but Dave and Jenny thought she was much too shaken to do anything other than go to sleep on their sofa, so they fed her a strong drink and tucked her in.

Chapter 33

About at hour before dawn Sunday morning, Pastor Brown had a brain-storm. It wasn't right for his daughter, Carmen, and her friend Natasha to get away. His protest march may be off but he could regain some of his pride by preventing Carmen and Natasha from being in the Road March later today. The more he thought about it the more he liked the idea. He got out of bed, dressed, told his wife he was going out for a short while and got into his car and drove over to Carmen's

Carmen fought against waking, but the insistent ringing of the door-bell finally got her up. She was a light sleeper. Her carnival-lover however slept on. There was no sound from Natasha or her companion in the next bedroom either. The door-bell kept ringing. Angrily, wondering who could be visiting at such an ungodly hour, and still foggy from too little sleep, she struggled into her robe and stumbled to the living room. A peep through the 'peep-hole' of the front door revealed her irate father.

The sight of his harsh features brought her fully awake. What was he up to? she thought with alarm. Or had something happened to her mother...?

Cautiously she opened the door but kept the 'security-chain' on. "What is it?" her tone was soft and subdued, barely more than a frightened whisper.

"One way or another a comin' in to get yours an' yu friend's Road March costume," he hissed through the narrow opening, eyes blazing.

"Yu... you an' yu friend ruin my plans. I want even a small revenge. Yu can make it easy on yourself by bringing me the costumes."

Carmen was greatly relieved he wasn't bringing bad news of her mother. Embarrassment at what she had done to him yesterday caused her to lower her eyes and wonder if she shouldn't give in to his request.

"Well, must I break down the door? If I have to do that I am goin' to let you feel my hand as well!"

Carmen knew she couldn't let down her Road March cell by allowing her dad to take away her costume. But she could assuage his pride and ease her guilt a bit by fooling him into thinking he had won. First, though, there were things she should say. "Dad," she said, "I am sorry about yesterday but I had to do it. I now know you love me" — she looked up into his eyes beseechingly — "and I love you."

His features softened, but only for a small moment. "You don't know love, yu Jezebel!" He snarled. "Go get those costumes before I break down the door and give you the beating of your life!"

"Yes." Involuntarily she flinched backward, tone subdued, eyes full of fear and grief. She was scared of the prospect of him beating her in such a foul temper, knowing he could squash her, Natasha, and their lovers with one hand. She left the door on its security-chain and went to fetch hers and Natasha's costumes from the previous year's Road March. Pastor wouldn't know the difference, she thought as she returned with the bird-like costumes.

To seal the trick she pleaded unconsciously: "Daddy, please, don't do this. My cell won't stand a chance of winning a prize. Can't you see your protest march would have ruined your church? I did you a good deed. Please..."

He had heard enough and was pleased with her remorse. He interrupted harshly, "Jus' hand over the costumes!"

She obeyed. He glared at the two colourful costumes and snarled "Devils work! I shall give them fire!" And with one last glower at the teary-eyed Carmen he left feeling much better than he had since yesterday.

Carmen wished she and Natasha hadn't done what they did yesterday. Dear God, she prayed, how am I ever going to convince him of my love?

With a sobbing sigh she thought: At least he thinks he won a bit of revenge.

Sunday morning saw Harry's wife in St. Mary getting ready for her trip to the Road March in Kingston, eager to catch Harry and return him to where he belonged. Home in her bed, between her strong thighs. Her ropes had been packed from last night. She left home with a small travelling bag over her shoulder and her 'supple-jack' stick in hand. The spirits told her she'd find Harry watching the Road March somewhere near the Half-Way-Tree Square.

In Kingston, Harry awoke at eight feeling refreshed. He had come home at one o'clock, after seeing his go-go escort to her home. His plans for Jenny foremost in his mind. From this afternoon until Friday he was going to drive Jenny crazy with fuck — hard ones — and all sort of punishment.

Now that the 'big day' was here he was feeling like a youth of twenty-five. In just five hours or so he would be knocking out Jenny's uptown boy, then flogging Jenny all the way to Kencot. Three days as his prisoner would be enough to give her the shakes for life, but he intended to keep her longer.

With a gleeful laugh, Harry began to prepare breakfast — coffee laced with rum, four eggs and half of a two pound loaf of bread.

Jenny and Dave sighed with relief when, after Paula's seven o'clock departure, the radio announced that Pastor Brown had cancelled his protest march. Still Jenny and Dave were appreciative about the possible danger still surrounding the Road March. They remained in a funk till a ten o'clock news-flash announced that a joint police/military raid on 2 East Kingston ghettoes had just wiped out and captured all but a few of two gangs who had been preparing to attack Central police station and the General Penitentiary when the Road March began. The notorious Don J and several foreigners were amongst the dead. No security personnel had died but fifteen were wounded.

Upon hearing this news flash, Dave and Jenny regained their carnival spirit. They began last minute preparations for the midday start of the Road March.

Just before eleven o'clock that morning Bette got a call from the cops telling her what she had already guessed. The kidnap threat had been a hoax, Don J had been behind it and his death meant she was free to enter the Road March. Bette immediately called Joan, Anette and Dorret to give them the good news.

Eleven o'clock saw Jodi and Carl, dressed in their Road March costumes, driving to the starting point of the Road March on Constant Spring Road, at the Constant Spring Golf Club. They arrived just behind Jenny and Dave.

Carl glowed at the sight of Jenny. Here was the black bitch, he thought, who was going to make it possible for him to win Jodi's unconditional love. As Jodi had advised him, he was going to make his move when they were past Half-Way-Tree.

Chapter 34

The Sunday morning had began with very dark overcast sky. But by noon the sky was fairly clear, a rosy sun moving in and out of light-grey clouds. It was minutes before 12.30 when the first of the twelve costumed groups set off behind the first 'music-truck'.

There was a huge crowd at the starting point — to cheer off the eye-catching, colourful and sexually clad groups. The 'whining', 'prancing' costumed groups and the accompanying calypso - blasting music-trucks were a sight to behold as the March moved down the pedestrian lined street.

The previous year's big Road March had been the first most Jamaicans had seen and it pulled a huge crowd. Before 1990, Carnival and Road March was a thing done in quiet residential avenues of upper-middle class areas. This year it was as if all of Jamaica was out on the Road March route. They jammed the sidewalks, crammed the roofs of buildings, homes and business places dancing, waving, cheering, oblivious of the hot midday sunshine. Onlookers and costumed revellers alike pulsed and crackled with sensuality and life. The air hummed with soca. Cops along the route forgot about security and got caught up in the joyous bacchanal of music and desire.

Even the many female onlookers who were disappointed with the low percentage of males in the Road March got caught up in the excitement.

The mood was infectious and all of Jamaica glowed with Carnival Fever.

When the Road March began, Pastor Brown and his wife were on their way home after a morning of Sunday School and 10 o'clock service. Attendance had been good, as usual, and nobody seemed angry that Pastor had called off the protest march.

Their journey home from their Molynes Road church didn't take Pastor and Mrs. Brown anywhere near the Road March route. Mrs. Brown was grateful that the protest march was off. Pastor had told her it was 'The Spirit' which told him to call off the protest march. He said he had a vision while driving on Saturday. The sulky spirits in which he had returned home Saturday afternoon, was due he claimed to Carmen summoning him on an alleged 'spiritual matter' which had turned out to be her usual rant about his church being false.

Mrs. Brown had no reason to disbelieve her husband.

Pastor was remorseful over having lied about 'The Spirit', but he was sure the Lord would forgive him. There was forgiveness for all sins; and the Lord had commanded man to love his wife as he loved the church. So he had lied to save his wife from a life-time of heart-break over their daughter's sacrilegious treachery.

At least, Pastor mused, Carmen and Natasha wouldn't be in the Road March since he had burned their costumes. Perhaps one day in the week he'd even visit them as a sign of his forgiveness and love.

The widowed Mrs. Hurt and Cedric were at Cedric's house comforting Mrs. Hurt's two sons at the loss of their father.

Cedric had withdrawn from the Road March to be with his 'new family'. Now that Mr Hurt was dead, Cedric was determined to win the boys' love.

Mrs. Hurt was ashamed of it, but she couldn't help thinking her husband's death was a blessing. No need now for a divorce, and she and Cedric would have the boys to themselves.

At the time that the Road March began, Inspector Hinds and Supt. Mills were being congratulated by the Commissioner on the success of the morning's joint military/police operations. The Inspector's wife and daughters were in the Road March.

Carmen and Natasha were in the first group of the Road March.

They were enjoying themselves, tingling with sensuality like every-body else. They were actually proud, having forced Pastor to call off his protest march, having temporarily laid aside their self-disgust at the method they had used to force his hand. They hoped Pastor wouldn't spot them on television and realise that the costumes Carmen had given him that morning had nothing to do with this year's Road March; they desperately wanted him to believe he had kept them out of the Road March, reasoning that that would make it easier for a reconcilia-tion between him and Carmen.

Unfortunately for him, shortly after arriving home from church, Pas-tor turned on the television out of curiousity only, to see a close up of Carmen and Natasha clad in skimpy costumes, whining down Half-Way-Tree Road. He came close to cursing lewdly for the first time in some thirty years.

Jenny and Dave, Carl and Jodi, Bette and her two 'Troopers' (Joan and Anette), Dorret and Donna were all in the third cell of the sixth group of the Road March. Their costumes were African-inspired in design — warriors and dancing girls. All the men and some of the la-dies were in warrior gear consisting of micro leather skirts and leather breast-plates. They carried tall and colourful shields made of card-board, and spears painted and bamboo tipped with sharp pointed wooden heads.

Jenny was one of the dancing girls. She sported a long print skirt and scanty top. Her wrists, ankles and neck were decorated with colourful beads. A headwrap matched her skirts. Like most of her fellow revellers, Jenny's feet were in expensive canvas shoes and she wore her costume over gym wear. Her face, was painted with bold streaks of colourful make-up.

Harry decided that the crowds were too thick in the Mandela Park area of Half-Way-Tree Square. So he crossed over to the Half-Way-Tree Road section of the route where it would be easier to grab Jenny when she passed by. It also placed him nearer to Kencot.

Deep in his own scheme, Harry hadn't noticed his wife following him. His heart raced at the sound of the approaching Road March and his head was mellow from the Q of rum he had had not long ago. His whip, a plaited leather one was tucked into his pants. There were also a pair of hand-cuffs in his pants pocket. His black face shone with anticipation.

Harry's wife had sensed him all morning but hadn't spotted him until he left Mandela Park. She was damn sorry the crowds seemed too thick for lassoing, but getting close to him would be easy. She followed him down the crowded sidewalk of Half-Way-Tree Road. Her tall two hundred and fifty pound bulk moving with agility, the approaching Road March bearing down behind her.

The music seemed to be heralding the victory she tasted at hand. She felt herself getting aroused and wet at the thought of Harry returning to their matrimonial bed after all these years. Her fleshy dark-brown face was a picture of ecstasy.

She caressed the oily 'supple-jack' rod in her hand.

Her ropes were in the bag over her shoulder. It occurred to her that it would be a nice touch to put off jumping Harry until his eyes were filled with the Road March.

So when he stopped by Holy Childhood High she ducked out of sight and passed behind to take up a position below him. Close but not very close. She smiled, watching him watch for the costumed revellers' entry onto Half-Way-Tree Road. Wouldn't be long now. It sounded as if the leading music-truck and group were entering the Constant Spring Road section of Half-Way-Tree Square.

The leading group of Road Marchers and music-truck ground to a halt at Mandela Park as they came up against the dense crowds there. The predominantly middle-class revellers found themselves getting free refreshments from the ghetto vendors - oranges , bag juices and coconuts. A touching reality. After a while several uniformed cops returned to earth long enough to good-naturedly get the crowds to move back. The Road March surged forward once more.

When the sixth group was alongside Mandela Park, Jodi pressed her sweaty body to Carl's and whispered in his ear "Half-Way-Tree Road coming up."

Carl nodded his acknowledgment, firmly gripping his spear and readying himself for the attack. When their group moved onto Half-Way-Tree Road, Carl moved closer to Jenny and kept by her side. Soon...

Dave was now circled by Bette, Joan and Anette. Jenny unprotected.

Carl thought it was a good moment to make his move, but then Jenny suddenly veered away from him and Dave broke free from Bette,

171

Joan and Anette. Carl cursed his luck. Dave was now whining by Jenny's side. Next thing he knew he was swept aside by Dorret and Donna and two other girls. They bumped him, and spun and ground their sweating bodies into his.

The revellers, onlookers and the calypso music blended into one.

Upon nearing Holy Childhood High, Carl saw Dave dance away from Jenny. Carl danced over to Jenny seeing Jodi wink her encouragement. Any moment now, Carl thought, adrenaline filling his blood.

Harry spotted Jenny instantly and pulled the long plaited leather whip from inside his shirt with one hand, the hand-cuffs with the other. He bent low until Jenny whined pass his position, then he rose and trotted after her. He wasn't hearing the blasting soca from the nearest music-truck anymore. All his attention was riveted on Jenny.

Harry's wife was puzzled when she saw him pull out his whip and cuffs. For a moment she thought he was onto her, but then she saw him peering at the revellers and realised he was after some girl in the group coming up. She took out her lasso rope and when he trotted out into the costumed revellers, she followed. This was going to be even better than expected, she thought.

Dave caught sight of Harry and instinctively knew he was after Jenny who was ten feet to Dave's right. Dave dropped his shield and leapt towards Jenny, pushing aside startled group members.

At the moment that Carl whirled around to fake a stumble which would send his spear tragically into Jenny's eyes, Jodi was pushed against Jenny by Harry. Jenny stumbled aside from the impact and it was Jodi's face which confronted Carl. His spear however was already moving and he was unable to correct his thrust...

Jodi had no time to evade Carl's spear. The sharp wooden point dug into her cheek, just missing her eye. She screamed, sure that she was blind. Blood filled her eye and streamed down her thick coat of make-up. She fainted, falling onto Jenny's bottom.

Carl dropped his spear and stood there gaping incredulously. Face ashen, eyes wide with disbelief.

Other revellers screamed at the sight.

At the moment that Jenny caught Jodi's limp body, Harry was reaching out to grab her. But in his eagerness he had forgotten about Dave.

In the split mili-second before his huge hand clamped Jenny's forearm, Harry was hit by two powerful blows: his wife's fat fist hammering down into his shoulder; and a powerful jab from Dave. Harry crumpled to his knees, whip and hand-cuffs falling from his hand. His right hand slid harmlessly down Jenny's arm. Jenny was shaken by Harry's appearance but she didn't let go of Jodi's limp body. Harry, who was seeing stars, felt a rope drop over his shoulders to pin his arms to his sides. Then a familiar voice froze him with terror. He'd know that rumbling voice anywhere.

"Alright youngman," Harry's wife said to Dave, "I av' him secure. I is him wife." And so saying, she dragged the speechless Harry off into Holy Childhood gateway. Hundreds cheered, having gladly given her a path to drag Harry through. They clustered around and howled their glee as the first of many 'supple-jack' lashes struck the pleading, well-tied Harry. What a Bangarang at Carnival!

The Road March had bogged down as revellers tried to understand what had happened.

By this time, Carl had regained enough of his wits to help carry the unconscious Jodi to the sidewalk where she was given first-aid.

Jenny's costume was smeared with Jodi's blood. Her eyes kept darting to the howling crowd around Harry and his wife. She knew Harry's fat wife was giving him a good dose of what he had intended for her. But she was sure Dave would've spoiled Harry's plan if the fat wife hadn't appeared.

The Road March resumed when Jodi was borne away on a stretcher. Carl went with her, thanking God her eye had been spared. The revellers seeing that Jodi was alright, quickly regained the tempo of carnival.

Jenny and Dave never suspected that Carl had intended to hurt Jenny. It would remain Jodi and Carl's secret.

In the meantime, a well-bound aching and trembling Harry was being hustled into a taxi by his grinning wife.

She was squeezing his crotch with a hungry gleam in her eyes as the taxi drove away from Half-Way-Tree Square. Harry was cold and silent with dread. Over in New Kingston Jenny was kissing Dave, in time to the sweet soca music.

Aftermath

It's now over a year after the 1991 Carnival Week. Christmas is near. 1993 Carnival Week is already being anticipated.

The red-headed prisoner who the late Don J had intended to free from Central police station lock-up, turned out to be a highly wanted gangster on the wanted lists of the F.B.I., the French and the Italian police. Don J's surmise was correct: the prisoner had had a recent 'face-job' and had passports and drivers licences to match his new face.

Detective Inspector Hinds is now a Superintendent. He also got a National award for the part he played in nabbing Don J. He has given up all thoughts of resisting his wife's body. But he has stopped taking 'tainted' money, having made some wise investments which are about to begin paying off handsomely. He will be able to satisfy his wife's desires for more luxury, using 'honest' earnings.

Mrs. Hurt and Cedric got married in September 1992. Her sons have grown fond of Cedric.

Pastor Brown and his wife are into 'spanking' as a sex game. She finally got up the courage to tell him she didn't mind being spanked and enjoyed the passion he always showed after using the 'holy-belt'. He has put aside the holy-belt which he only uses for special occasions.

He now uses a light velvet wrapped paddle and they have 'wild-nights' twice per week.

Carmen and Natasha are still embarrassed by the memory of seeing Pastor Brown's nakedness. They are still 'wracking' their brains for a way to soften Pastor's cold attitude towards them.

Carmen no longer doubts that Pastor loves her as much as her friends' fathers love them, and she is making a Christmas card expressing her love for him. She isn't sure that saving the Road March from the protest march was worth the new distance between them but she is sure her plan saved his career from ruin.

Bette now has a larger Troop — old 'Troopers' Joan and Anette, and their three carnival lovers, plus a black young lady doctor and her black fiancé. Bette is the undisputed leader and she knows how to boss the men without their being aware of it. Her lover thinks she is Venus and Cleopatra rolled into one. He is a handsome quadroon who Bette thinks has the loveliest eyes.

Bette, Joan and Anette no longer look down on blacks without a college degree. And they hope to get Dave and Jenny to join their circle.

Dorret and Donna are happy. Their parties are a favourite with the city's lesbian society. Dorret still works alongside Bette, Joan and Anette. They all lunch together as before and Dorret visits their homes occasionally. But, all in all, Dorret is no longer a Trooper.

Dorret is sure Dave could never have made her as happy as Donna does.

Dorret's father is still amused over Dorret's new lifestyle. His wife copes by pretending she doesn't know Dorret and Donna are lovers.

Jodi's cheek has a slight scar. Despite the best doctors in Jamaica and the U.S., the muscle damage has left her with a twisted mouth and a squinting eye, although her sight is fine. As expected, she has completely lost all self-esteem with the loss of her pretty looks. She has a persistent twitch and wears huge sunglasses night and day. Her former fiancé dropped her. She and Carl will be marrying in January.

Jodi doesn't love Carl but she is sure no one else will marry her, and the thought of being a spinster frightens her to near insanity.

Carl still loves Jodi and feels he owes her his life. He doesn't see her new unattractive face, only the old beautiful one of the pictures he has hidden.

Jodi dislikes seeing pictures of her former beauty. Still, she is on a strict diet and does daily exercise to keep her body in shape. And she has one joy — sex.

She and Carl almost never go out and they never discuss Jenny or Road March '91 for that matter.

Harry's wife kept him tied up for over a week, during which time she rode him night and day. 'Juiced' him of years of vitality.

Now he quietly goes from home to work at various construction sites about the parish and his little farm. He drinks at home and has become a loner. He has no energy for other women. He is convinced that if he went to the moon, his wife would come fetch him back. He is resigned to his fate, and looking forward to old-age when she won't be able to demand sex anymore.

Jenny has found that she has a talent for writing fiction and Dave has encouraged her to take up a correspondence short-story writing course. He bought her several books about novel writing. They have agreed not 'to try' for any babies until after Jenny has done two years of serious writing.

They will be going to Africa for their second honeymoon, and indeed they are looking forward to this year's carnival and the first blow out.